BIGGLES' CHINESE PUZZLE

Eight stories of how Biggles and his friends,
Algy, Ginger and Bertie, expose sinister
rackets in smuggling; snatch luminous
clay from a sinking rock; sort out the
connection between an old picture and an
old plane; track down a parson who
indulged in strange extra-parochial
activities; and probe the secrets of an
unorthodox mental hospital.

Biggles at his swiftest and surest.

CAPTAIN W. E. JOHNS

BIGGLES' CHINESE PUZZLE

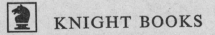

KNIGHT BOOKS

the paperback division of Brockhampton Press

ISBN 0 340 04016 5

This edition first published 1967 by Knight Books,
the paperback division of Brockhampton Press Ltd, Leicester
Third impression 1970

Printed and bound in Great Britain by
Cox & Wyman Ltd, London, Reading and Fakenham

First published in Great Britain by Brockhampton Press Ltd 1955

CONTENTS

Publisher's Note

Readers will understand that since this book was originally written, the political situation, and currency values, in the Far East have changed very much, and are still changing. Scientific progress has made enormous advancement, and geographical boundaries have altered. But we feel that this will not affect in any way the enjoyment of the stories.

1

BIGGLES'
CHINESE PUZZLE

'GET me the Paris Sûreté on the private line. I want to speak to Marcel Brissac. He promised to let me have some Interpol* figures weeks ago and I haven't heard a word since.' Biggles gave the order to police pilot Ginger Hebblethwaite.

Ginger went to the instrument and put in the call. In a minute he was through. 'It's Joudrier here,' he told Biggles. 'I think you'd better speak to him.'

Biggles took the receiver. '*Bon jour, mon vieux. Ici* Bigglesworth,' he greeted. And that was all he said for a long time. So long did he sit with the receiver to his ear, and so dark became his frown as he listened, that it was evident to all those in the Special Air Police Office at Scotland Yard that something was wrong.

At long last he hung up. 'Marcel's missing. He's been missing for six weeks,' he announced briefly.

'Six *weeks*!' exclaimed Algy.

Biggles nodded. 'Looks bad,' he averred, grimly.

'Has Joudrier any idea of what he was doing when he failed to report back at headquarters?'

*International Police Commission.

'Yes. Or he knew what he was trying to do. That's what he's just been telling me.'

'But what's Joudrier doing about it?'

'Nothing, apparently. He says there's nothing he can do.'

'That's nonsense,' burst out Ginger.

Biggles shrugged. 'It's all very well to say that. There are four of us here. As you know, Marcel has to work on his own.'

'What's the French Air Force doing?'

'Fighting thugs in Indo-China, trying to keep order in North Africa, and policing France's colonial empire. I imagine they've plenty on their plate without looking for a stray cop.'

'What did Joudrier tell you, old boy?' inquired Bertie Lissie.

'He said it was known there had been some big-scale currency smuggling between France and Indo-China, and Marcel, who was convinced that aircraft came into the picture, flew out to Saigon hoping to get a line on it. Nothing's been heard of him since. It's only recently that Joudrier became alarmed. Naturally, he wouldn't expect regular reports from Marcel while he was working on a job of that sort.'

'What exactly has been going on?' asked Algy.

'Apparently some of the big business merchants in Saigon have been making enormous profits out of the war in Indo-China. They've got more local currency than is healthy for them, or they know what to do with, so they've been paying forty piastres, which is six hundred and eighty francs, for the American dollar. The dollar, in Paris, is worth about four hundred francs. So it's a matter of simple arithmetic. If you can buy a dollar in France for four hundred francs, and sell it in Saigon for six hundred and eighty, you're making a profit of two hundred and eighty francs. That's on one dollar. Multiply it by ten thousand and your profit is nearly three million francs – say, three thousand pounds. Easy, isn't it? Of course, there's one snag.'

'Getting the dollars to Saigon,' murmured Ginger.

'Exactly. Joudrier doesn't know how, but apparently that was, and still is, being done. Marcel suspected aircraft, which could carry millions of dollars in paper money. It begins to look as if he was right, too. I'd say he got on the track, and found himself up against something bigger than he could handle. There will always be service men who try to make a bit on the side by currency exchange, but that's only chicken feed, and most governments turn a blind eye to it. But when it comes to trafficking in millions the thing becomes serious, and they have to do something.'

'The question is, what are *we* going to do about it?' put in Ginger.

'It's hard to see how we can do anything. Indo-China is France's worry.'

'But Marcel is a member of Interpol. So are we. Don't tell me that members can be bumped off while the rest wash their hands and say it's nothing to do with them.'

'I'll have a word with the Air Commodore about it,' decided Biggles. 'I know what he'll say before I go. He'll be reluctant to interfere in a French domestic problem.'

'But look here, old boy: who says it's a French domestic problem?' protested Bertie. 'These racketeers might be of any nationality. They might even be operating from British territory.'

Biggles shook his head. 'Could be, but I think that's unlikely. Get the thing clear. There's no law in Indo-China against converting piastres into francs, and it's legal for francs to be returned to France. The illegal part is the smuggling of hard currency notes out of France into Saigon. Aside from that, currency operations on a big scale defeat the very object for which currency control was introduced. Of course, for all we know these francs may be converted into other currencies; but that's surmise. Had Marcel thought that sterling came into the picture surely he would have told us before he set off on what he must have known was a dangerous mission. These big money merchants stick at nothing, because they're breaking the law anyway and stand to make or lose a packet.'

'Never mind the arithmetic,' argued Bertie. 'The basic idea of Interpol was that one member country should help another. If they're not going to do that then the whole bally thing falls down. If Marcel is in a jam then it's up to us to get him out.' Adjusting his eyeglass he looked around for support.

'You may have something there,' admitted Biggles. 'But it isn't a matter of what we would *like* to do. It's a matter of what we're *allowed* to do. We're not free agents. The government pays our wages, and to be fair they've allowed us plenty of scope, for which reason I'm not going to embarrass anybody by gate-crashing into French territory.' He got up. 'I'll see what the Chief has to say,' he concluded.

He was away for perhaps half an hour, and his expression, when he returned, was non-committal. 'I haven't done too badly,' he announced, resuming his seat. 'As I expected, the Air Commodore nearly swallowed his tonsils when I suggested that we ought to try to find out what has happened to Marcel. He didn't want to listen to any argument, but eventually I talked him round to the point where he's agreed to ring up the French Embassy, the Currency Commission, and the rest of them.'

'All he'll do is get himself snarled up in a lot of red tape,' declared Algy.

'Probably. Anyhow, I've done my best. There was no question of our pushing off to the Far East on our own account. I've told the Chief we're willing to go, although, even if he gives us the okay, I'm by no means clear as to what we could do. Indo-China is French. To complicate matters there's a war on, with, as far as I can make out, half a dozen different armies fighting anybody and everybody. What excuse are we going to give for barging in? Of course, Indo-China is only one end of the racket. There's another end somewhere; probably in France or in French North Africa. But we'll talk about that if the question arises. Meanwhile we'll rest on our oars until the Air Commodore is given a decision.'

This came about an hour later, when the Air Commodore entered. 'All right,' he said shortly. 'You may go – with limitations. Obviously, you can't operate as British police officers, so you'll be provided with papers showing that you're civilians on a trade mission. You'll fly a civilian aircraft, on charter. Make your own arrangements to keep in touch with Joudrier at the Sûreté, and finally, don't be away too long. I may need you here. For heaven's sake be careful what you get up to. If you get in a mess with any of the several forces now playing for power in the Far East, don't rely on me to get you out. The business is to find Marcel – or find out what happened to him. Don't get tangled up in the war, or anything connected with it. That's all. Good luck.' The Air Commodore went out.

Biggles looked at the others. 'That's fair enough,' he observed. 'Now we know where we are we'd better do some hard thinking. We don't want to make the same mistake as Marcel seems to have done, although we can only work on the same lines.'

'What are they?' asked Algy.

'He went to Saigon, where the dirty work is being done. As I said just now that's one end of the black market. Where the other end is we don't know, and I doubt if Marcel knew. He may have made some inquiries before he went, but I don't think he could have picked up anything important or he'd have told Joudrier.'

'And what would he have done in Saigon?'

'As he suspected the racket was being worked by aircraft he would obviously go to the airport to check up on the 'planes using it. That's what we shall have to do. It's no use walking about the streets. Marcel may have pressed his inquiries too hard and let it become known that he was a police agent. We shall play our parts as a trade mission. I shall be merely the pilot of the aircraft, and Ginger my mechanic. That will give us an excuse for hanging about the airfield. You two will have to put up some sort of show of buying or selling something. That's a detail that can be settled later. In one way our nationality should be an advantage. I mean, what business would British police officers have in Indo-China? But let's get mobile. You start to get the machine ready and dig out all the information available about official civil aircraft using the airport, although I don't think the regular air liners are being used by the gang because that would mean the customs officials were involved. I'm going to dash over to Paris and have a word with Joudrier. Ring him, Ginger, and tell him I'm on my way. I shan't be long.'

Three hours later Biggles was in the office of Captain Joudrier, head of the Department of the Paris police headquarters to which Marcel was attached.

He found the detective in a state of indecision, because, as Joudrier explained, he had no actual information to suggest that something tragic had happened, and was, therefore, reluctant to start a scare that might not only turn out to be a false alarm, but could make things dangerous for Marcel should he be on a hot scent. Nevertheless, he could not ignore the fact that it was unlike Marcel to remain silent for so long. All he knew was, and this is what worried him, Marcel's Morane was not at the airport. It had been there, but had gone.

'And you have no idea of what he intended to do when he got to Saigon?' queried Biggles.

'He didn't know himself. He told me that. His inquiries at this end provided no definite information. That was why he went to Saigon.'

'What inquiries did he make here?'

'He didn't say, from which I imagine they were merely a matter of routine.'

'Have you examined his desk for possible notes that might provide a clue as to his intentions?'

Joudrier shrugged. 'Surely he would take any such notes with him.'

'One would think so,' agreed Biggles. 'There's a chance that he may have made some marks on a map in working out a particular compass course, for example. That would give us an idea of the ground he intended to cover.'

'We will look,' said Joudrier, getting up and leading the way to Marcel's office.

For a time it seemed as if his supposition was correct. Everything had been left neat and tidy. There were no maps of Indo-China, Marcel, apparently, having taken them with him, as was to be expected. His diary ended on the day of his departure. The scribbling pad, beside which lay a ball-pointed pen, was topped by a sheet of plain paper.

'You see,' said Joudrier. 'If he made notes he either destroyed them or took them with him.'

'If he made them with that pen the impression might have gone through to the next sheet,' Biggles pointed out, carefully removing the blank page and holding it up to the light. 'Yes, I think there's something here,' he went on. 'It's too faint to be read as it is, but we should be able to make it legible.'

'Bring it along,' requested Joudrier.

Back in his office a light dusting with black carbon powder was all that was necessary to throw the writing into white relief. It consisted of five names and addresses, although no town or country was given.

'What do you make of it?' asked Biggles.

'These,' said Joudrier slowly, 'are the names of Paris business houses that trade with the Far East and have offices in Saigon. Or to be correct, three of them are. The other two are Saigon companies with offices in Paris – which comes to much the same thing.'

'From the name, one of them appears to be a Chinese concern.'

'Yes. Ching Loo and Co. They're well-known Oriental merchants with offices in every big Eastern city. They own a lot of property in Saigon, including the Pagoda Palace Hotel. I'm afraid we shan't learn much from these.'

'Why, I wonder, did Marcel make a note of them?'

Joudrier lifted a shoulder. 'Who knows? He may have intended to stay at the Pagoda Palace.'

'Since he evidently thought it worth while to note these names I'll take a copy,' said Biggles.

'Would you like me to provide you with special police passes?' suggested Joudrier helpfully. 'They might be useful in an emergency.'

Biggles shook his head. 'No thanks. They might be dangerous, so I wouldn't risk using them. With all respect to you, there might be an official in the plot – even a policeman. In this sort of business, when it's big enough, money has been known to corrupt even the best men. It's better to trust nobody.'

'Yes, my friend, I'm afraid you are right,' conceded Joudrier sadly.

And on that note the conversation ended, Biggles telling his French colleague that he would keep in touch with him as far as possible but would refrain from calling on him for help unless it was vitally necessary.

He took a taxi to the airport and by six o'clock was back in his own office.

*

Ten days later the old but still serviceable Air Police Halifax was making its approach to the airport of Saigon under a leaden sky. Below lay the Mekong River, its waters grey, its muddy banks merging into the great shapeless areas of scrub and forest in which a million men, white, black, brown and yellow, were fighting an apparently futile and interminable war.

The machine landed in pouring rain. The first hour on the ground was spent in refuelling, finding accommodation for the aircraft and going through the usual tedious formalities; and in this respect, Ginger noted, there was nothing slack about the way the French customs officials went about their business. The 'samples' of textiles which the party had brought as part of the set-up of the trade organization were examined closely. However, at the finish they were 'cleared'.

'Now what's the drill?' asked Algy.

'Get a taxi, taking all the kit with you, and see about rooms. You might try the place that was on Marcel's list – the Pagoda Palace. There's a chance he went there, so we might pick up some news. Ginger, if only as a matter of courtesy, I think you'd better report our arrival at the British Legation. I'll follow on.'

'What are you going to do?'

'I'm going to have a mooch round the hangars just to make sure Marcel's Morane isn't here. It could have come in while we were on the way out – not that I think there's much hope of that. However, I'll have a look. After that – well, I don't know. It's a bit hard to know where to start. I'll see you at the hotel.'

So they parted.

Biggles knew, when he had said it was a bit hard to know where to start, that this was an understatement. Although he had been turning the matter over in his mind during the long hours in the air on the way out, he still had no definite plan. To make inquiries openly about the missing aircraft would, if there had been foul play, not only defeat their object but put them in a position of some danger. Apart from learning how the smuggling was being done by watching incoming and outgoing aircraft, all he could hope for was, as they were on the spot, some rumour or whisper of gossip which would put them on the track.

He had not taken more than a dozen paces towards the exit that gave them access to the tarmac when, to his surprise, he was accosted by a youngish man who sat on one of the seats reading a newspaper.

'Hello there. You an American?' was the question, cheerfully put.

'No. Sorry to disappoint you. I'm British,' answered Biggles.

'Too bad. Funny, when you're a long way from home, how you jump at the chance of having a say-so with someone from your own country.'

'I gather you're an American.'

'Sure am. I should have known you were British by that antiquated crate you brought in.'

Biggles smiled. 'Yes, she's a bit of an old stager, but she still gets around.'

'I saw plenty of 'em when I was in England during the war, but I'd have thought they'd all have been on the scrap heap by now.'

'When they became obsolete the government sold them at a price that made them worth converting for long distance charter work.'

The American nodded. 'What you doing in this dump?'

'Brought out a couple of chaps who are hoping to sell a new line in wool shirts and pants.'

The American grinned. 'What a hope!'

'What are you doing here?' inquired Biggles. 'Something to do with the war?'

'Not me, brother. I've had all the war I want. I'm a delivery pilot under the American Aid Plan. Bring new kites out and take old ones back for reconditioning.'

'To America?'

'Nope. Wouldn't be worth it. As far as Marseilles. We've a repair depot there.'

'Must be tough going.'

'Sure is. Just plain bus driving. Waste of time and money, of course. These hamfisted Orientals break the stuff up as fast as they get it. The 'planes don't cost 'em anything and it keeps me in a job, so who cares? It's the waiting about in this cock-eyed dump that kills me.'

'You mean, you do this run on your own?'

'No. There are four of us, but it ain't often we're in one place together. I've got a navigator. He spends the time between trips drinking himself to death. There's nothing else to do. How about one?'

'Not at the moment, thanks. I want to give my machine the once-over and get my bearings.'

'Where are you staying?'

'Pagoda Palace.'

'It's as good as anywhere. That's where I sleep.'

'May see you there.'

'Okay.'

Biggles walked on. It was on the tip of his tongue to ask the easy-going American if he had seen anything of a Morane; but he thought better of it. He might ask him when he knew him better. Pondering the matter he perceived that he had already discovered one air link between Indo-China and Europe that was not on his list. No doubt there were others. He spent two hours wandering about the airport, but although he looked in every hangar he did not find Marcel's Morane. He was tempted to question some of the mechanics, but refrained. When air liners came in or departed he watched the customs procedure without seeing anything in the slightest degree suspicious. It all seemed to be normal and straightforward.

He was on his way to call a taxi when the American reappeared. 'Do you spend the day here?' asked Biggles curiously.

'Yep. I have to wait here for orders. Never know when a job's coming my way. Looks like we shall have to postpone that drink, pal. I'm pushing out in the morning, in an old Douglas.'

'For Marseilles?'

'Sure.'

'Hope it keeps fine for you.' Biggles walked on, a slight frown on his face, for it seemed to him that the young American had already had plenty to drink. However, that was no affair of his. He wasn't the only pilot to drink more than normal thirst demanded.

Biggles took a cab to the Pagoda Palace where he found the others installed.

'Any news?' asked Ginger.

'None,' answered Biggles. 'I had a word with an American who's ferrying for the American Aid people, but I didn't ask leading questions. He stays here. He seems a decent chap, but be careful if he gets you at the bar. He's already had plenty to drink. Let him do the talking. He's in the mood. Let's see about something to eat.'

Feeling a bit strained after the long journey, it was Biggles' intention to retire early. Before doing so,

however, he spent a little while going through the hotel
visitors' book. From this he learned that the name of
the American ferry pilot was Bollard. He then found
the date on which Marcel had booked in. He had booked
out three days later, but this entry, Biggles noted, was
not in Marcel's handwriting. The ink was of a slightly
different colour, too, from that in the ink-well, which
most people had used. Who had made the entry, he
wondered. Whoever it was, the writer must have known
that Marcel was not coming back, which implied that
he was aware of his fate.

This looked bad, and it was with fading hopes that
Biggles returned to the others, in the lounge, to tell them
that he was going to turn in. He had just advised them
to do the same when the American came through the
swing doors. He walked straight over and it was clear
from his easy familiarity and a slight slur in his speech
that he had been trying to relieve his boredom at the
bar. But this is not to say that he was drunk.

'How about a drink?' he suggested, in a manner that
was friendly enough.

Rather than risk hurting the man's feelings Biggles
accepted. 'Which way do you travel when you go?' he
asked nonchalantly.

'Straight as I can make it. Bangkok, Calcutta,
Karachi, Baghdad, Cairo. I've done the trip so many
times I could do it with my eyes shut,' boasted Bollard.
'With no reason to hurry I can take my time.'

'I imagine you get hung up occasionally, anyway,
when you run into airport red tape,' prompted Biggles.

'Me? Not on your life. On this job we carry diplomatic
passes, issued at the highest level; and believe me,
brother, no one in his right mind would get in our way.'

Bollard grinned. 'Working for the cause of humanity makes us kinda important.'

'And having sweated all the way to Marseilles you turn round and come back. Don't you get a bit tired of it?'

'No more than the guys who fly the regular services. Besides which I'm practically my own boss. I don't have to stick to a fixed schedule. I'm better paid, and, naturally, a guy can always make a dollar or two on the side.' Bollard winked.

'Naturally,' agreed Biggles dryly.

As if he had realized that he had been indiscreet Bollard switched the subject. 'How do you find this place?'

'The town or the hotel?'

'The hotel.'

'Very good, as Eastern hotels go.'

'Should be. It's run by the Ching Loo outfit. They're the big noise here, and look like being bigger. Buying property everywhere. They'll soon own the whole goldarned city.' Bollard dropped his voice. 'I keep in with 'em because there's a whisper they're going to start their own air line. I aim to get in at the top when the war here folds up.'

'Do you mean you know this Mr. Ching Loo?'

'Not yet; but Estere, the Swiss manager here, has promised to fix a meeting. Ching Loo seldom leaves his big place in the country. If you're still here when I get back, which should be in a coupla weeks or so, I'll give you an intro to Estere. He's a useful guy to know.'

'Thanks a lot,' acknowledged Biggles.

'Think nothing of it.' Bollard finished his drink at a gulp. 'How about another?'

Biggles was saved from the embarrassment of having to decline by the arrival of a dark-skinned waiter, who whispered something in the American's ear.

'I shall have to be getting along,' stated Bollard, somewhat abruptly. 'So long. Be seeing you.'

Biggles' eyes followed him thoughtfully as he left the room.

'What do you make of him?' asked Algy softly.

'I don't know,' answered Biggles slowly. 'To our way of thinking he shoots a bit of a line about himself, but that's typical of that type of American. It may be true or it may be bluff. We can ignore that. He's young. He's bored, and he's had plenty to drink. My first impression, at the airport, was that he was a straight, likeable sort of chap. But now I'm beginning to wonder. He's obviously well in with this Ching Loo organization. There need be nothing wrong with that if, as he hinted, he's playing his cards for a job with them.'

'What do you think he meant by making a few dollars on the side? That didn't sound too healthy,' suggested Bertie.

Biggles shrugged. 'He may have meant it literally. He wouldn't be the first man, with the advantages of a diplomatic pass, to carry a few odds and ends that are not strictly permissible. R.A.F. officers have been known to do it – without regarding it as being criminal, which of course it is. At any rate, it's sailing near the wind.'

'You don't think he knows anything about Marcel?' put in Ginger.

'If he does then I'm no judge of men. As a pilot he wouldn't stand for seeing another pilot bumped off, or his machine sabotaged. The only doubts I have are, does he know what he's doing? I mean, on his own admission he's well in with this Ching Loo organization, and if they're not straight he may be in something deeper than he suspects. If he isn't now, he may be before he's finished with them – or they're finished with him. I'd like to see what he does and where he goes when he gets to Marseilles; but we can't go tearing back there, and I don't like the idea of sending a signal to Joudrier to watch him. But it's getting late. I'm going to roost.'

'What's the drill for tomorrow?' asked Algy.

'I shall go back to the airport, possibly in time to see Bollard take off. You and Bertie had better make a pretence of showing your samples, in case we're being watched. Ginger can come with me. See you in the morning.'

Deep in thought Biggles turned into the main corridor towards the lift that served the bedroom floors. As he did so a door opened and out came the man who a moment before had been under discussion. In his hand he carried a well-filled portfolio. Without seeing Biggles he walked briskly down the corridor, and at the far end disappeared round the corner.

In passing it Biggles looked at the door of the room from which he had emerged. On it had been painted in bold white letters the word: Private. And below, smaller, P. Estere.

Reaching his bedroom Biggles switched on the light, sat on the bed and lit a cigarette. He was thinking about what he had just seen. In the lounge Bollard had carried no luggage of any sort. He had received a message, obviously from the manager, for he had gone to his room. He had left it with a portfolio. The implication was, the portfolio would travel with him when he left Saigon in the morning. The bag, or its contents, belonged to

Estere. Anyhow, Estere knew what was in the bag. Did Bollard know? The bag was too slim to carry an object of any size or weight; but it would hold a lot of paper. A large sum in high denomination currency notes, for instance. Bollard was flying a shuttle service between Saigon and Marseilles. He had boasted of making a few dollars on the side. He flew under the protection of a diplomatic pass. Which meant that the bag would not be opened en route. And last, but not least, the name Ching Loo had been on Marcel's list. The Pagoda Palace belonged to Ching Loo. Marcel had gone to the hotel on his arrival at Saigon.

For half an hour Biggles sat smoking, hardly moving. At first he was conscious of a feeling of disappointment, for his first impression of Bollard had been a favourable one, and it now began to look as if he had been mistaken. But a doubt still lingered, and it was based, curiously enough, on the American's own confession of 'making a few dollars on the side'. No, decided Biggles. Had Bollard known that he was in a wholesale currency smuggling racket he would not have talked like that. In fact, it was unlikely that he would have said anything at all – unless he was a fool. Which he was not, for no one entrusts large sums of money to a fool. Looked at in that light, it seemed more likely that if in fact he was engaged in handling contraband, somebody was using him as a tool.

Still turning the matter over in his mind Biggles undressed and got into bed.

*

The following morning Biggles and Ginger set off early for the airport. It was a dull, muggy, cheerless sort of day, but it was not actually raining, although there was every indication that it would before the day was out.

The narrow rutted road, muddy and puddled, wandered across a landscape that turned a sullen face to the dismal sky. Jungle and forest, their outlines blurred by steamy mist, followed flat, marshy paddy fields, with here and there a dilapidated hut or villa. At intervals there were block-houses, the concrete weather-stained, mossy and weed-grown, reminders that the country was at war and had been so for several years. Some of them were thinly manned by coloured troops drawn from one or other of the French dominions. Ginger smiled reminiscently as occasionally he picked out the familiar white kepi of a Foreign Legionnaire.* Over all hung an atmosphere of weariness, of misery and fear. In short, it was a tropical country at its worst.

On arrival at the airport, after making a pretence of being interested in the meteorological report, Biggles chose a place from where, without being seen, they could watch Bollard's arrival and subsequent actions. This was of course their main purpose in being there, although Biggles also intended to check up on sundry machines using the airport, if any; for in view of what had happened he had not yet had time to do this to his satisfaction. He knew from the published time-tables the movements of the regular air liners; but these he regarded as being outside the range of his inquiries.

On the airfield, a Douglas D.C.3 was standing on the concrete apron in front of Number Two hangar.

'That must be the machine Bollard is flying to France,' observed Biggles.

*See *Biggles, Foreign Legionnaire*.

Shortly afterwards the American arrived, carrying the portfolio in one hand and an attaché-case, presumably containing his travelling kit, in the other. With a cheerful word and a smile to the officials who were standing about, he walked past them without stopping and so on to the Douglas.

'You see,' said Biggles, 'they all know him and what his job is, so they don't trouble to check his baggage. Of course, for all we know the duty officer at this hour may be in the racket, supposing there is one, in which Bollard is the operative agent. Anyway, from what we've just seen there's nothing to prevent him from walking through with any sort of light-weight contraband if he wanted to. Whether he's on the level or not, he wouldn't get away with that in Europe.'

They moved on slowly to a point from which they could see the end of the incident, Ginger supposing that nothing now remained but for the aircraft to take off on its long run to the West. Indeed, the signs pointed to this. Bollard joined a man who was standing by, presumably his partner on the flight, had a word with him and climbed aboard. The second man remained at the cabin door. The engines came to life and remained ticking over. The man at the door, Ginger supposed, would now get in; the engines would be run up and the Douglas would move off. This did not happen. The man at the door stood still, staring at the scrub that fringed the landing area some fifty or sixty yards distant. He looked at his watch. A minute passed. The engines were run up and allowed to settle down again. Bollard then reappeared at the cabin door. He, too, looked at the scrub, with an occasional glance in the direction of the airport buildings.

'What goes on?' murmured Ginger.

'Looks as if they're waiting for somebody.'

'Why wait there?'

'There's a road behind that scrub. It skirts this part of the airfield.'

'What's the road got to do with it?'

'Well, where the machine is standing would be a good place to wait for someone who didn't want to walk through the booking hall.'

Ginger stared at Biggles' face. 'You mean, he's waiting for a passenger?'

'He's obviously waiting for something.'

'That's a bit hot. Would he have the brass face to do a thing like that?'

'Because such a thing couldn't happen at London Airport doesn't mean it couldn't happen here. You saw how Bollard walked through Customs as if they didn't exist.'

'Maybe this is how Bollard makes his extra dollars, giving people a cheap lift home.'

'Could be. He's got plenty of room. But I suspect there's more to it than that. He could probably get permission to carry a passenger if he wanted to, always supposing that person was free to leave the country. But if the person was not free to leave it would be a different matter. It wouldn't do for him to be checked through the booking hall. He would have to slip aboard under the curtain – or, shall we say, out of the bushes. And there must be a lot of people here who would be glad to get out of this pestilential hole – if they could find a way.'

'Such as?'

Biggles shrugged. 'I could think of several. People

wanted by the police; people who dodged the immi-
gration laws to get in, and now want to get out;
deserters from the army. . . .'

Biggles broke off, for at this juncture a man, a white
man in dirty green denims, burst out of the scrub, and
crouching low close to the hangar raced towards the
aircraft. The two airmen also moved, as if it was for this
they had been waiting. Bollard disappeared inside. The
other, beckoning urgently, waited until he was joined
by the new arrival. He literally pushed him in, got in
himself and closed the door. The engines roared and the
machine moved forward.

Biggles lit a cigarette. 'Very interesting,' he said dryly.

'So now we know,' remarked Ginger.

'What do we know?'

'Bollard's a crook.'

'That may be a strong word for such evidence as we
have. Don't take too much for granted.'

'He must be crazy, anyway, risking his ticket, to take
a chance like that for a few dollars.'

'You're still jumping at conclusions. We don't *know*
it was for a few dollars, or even a lot of dollars. Maybe
it was for nothing at all.'

'I don't get it.'

'I'm still reluctant to change my first opinion of
Bollard. If he's a downright crook I'll never trust my
judgment again. There's a chance that his motive, in
doing what he has just done, was inspired by something
more powerful than money.'

'Is there anything more powerful?' inquired Ginger
cynically.

'Yes, sometimes. Patriotism. Comradeship. Even
nationalism in certain circumstances. The French are

waging their war here largely with the Foreign Legion. We've seen some of them about. The man who just slipped away in that aircraft was wearing green denims, which are part of the tropical kit of the Legion. I'd say he was a deserter, or a man with strong compassionate reasons for wanting to get home. There are quite a lot of Americans in the Legion; men fascinated by the life as it is shown on films made in Hollywood. They must get a nasty shock when they arrive here and face the facts, which, without the glamour and romance, are pretty grim – as we can see for ourselves. Some of them may stand up to it, but there are bound to be others who would give anything to get out. I don't know. I'm merely trying to put a possible construction on the incident we've just witnessed. Not that it's any concern of ours. It isn't likely to help us to find Marcel. We might as well have a look at our own machine as we're so close.'

'It doesn't say much for Bollard's character if he's prepared to side with deserters,' opined Ginger, as they walked on towards the hangar.

'On the face of it I'm bound to agree. But let us not be too righteous about it. Wouldn't you be tempted to offer a helping hand to one of your own countrymen who found himself up against it far from home in a foreign country?'

'It would depend on the time, the place and the man,' answered Ginger evasively. 'You always look on the bright side.'

'Because I've learned not to judge people without being sure of my facts. But let's forget it. I'm more concerned with what Bollard had in that portfolio than who occupies the spare seats in his aircraft.'

They walked on to the hangar that housed the

Halifax and found it as they had left it. The few airport hands moving about took no notice of them. Turning away Biggles said: 'Let's see what's in the next shed. I've been so taken up with Bollard that I haven't had time to make a thorough check.'

They walked on.

Occupying the front part of the hangar, and nearly filling it, was a Douglas D.C.4 displaying the insignia of Air Vietnam, the important air line owned partly by Air France and local companies. Biggles gave it no more than a cursory glance, and was about to turn away when something behind it caught his eye. Without speaking, but with a curious expression on his face, he walked forward. He stopped, staring: but still he did not speak.

Ginger, who had followed, was also staring. For there before them, painted in war-time camouflage style and carrying a Chinese hieroglyph for its registration mark, was a Morane aircraft. 'A Morane,' he exclaimed. 'But that isn't Marcel's machine,' he went on quickly. 'His was painted blue – or it was the last time I saw it.'

Biggles sniffed. He took a quick pace forward and put a hand on the engine cowling. 'She's warm,' he said softly. 'This engine was running not long ago.' He went closer to the fuselage, peered at it, and the face that he then turned to Ginger had lost a little of its colour. 'This is either Marcel's machine or its double,' he asserted, in a voice thin with suppressed excitement. 'The blue has been painted over. You can see it where the top coat has been scratched along the seams.'

'Blue may have been the standard colour for a batch of Moranes.'

'Even so, it would be mighty queer for two of them to

find their way here. And what's this one doing in Chinese ownership? I'm going to find out who it belongs to. That shouldn't be difficult. Let's find a mechanic.'

There was no need to look for one, for at this moment two men in overalls, one European and the other Chinese, arrived on the scene with what seemed unnecessary haste; and before Biggles could speak they were asking him, in vehement French, what he was doing, and at the same time telling him to leave the building.

Biggles raised a soothing hand. 'All right – all right,' he remonstrated, in the same language. 'There's no need to get excited. And as for what we're doing, is there anything remarkable about us being interested in an unusual aeroplane? We're pilots, and there's no notice up about this hangar being private.' As he spoke Biggles made his way slowly towards the open doors. 'Am I right in supposing that the little 'plane belongs to a local Chinese gentleman?' he questioned casually.

'This is a private hangar,' was the curt reply from the white man.

Perceiving that the men had no intention of answering questions, Biggles did not press them. Taking a cigarette from his case he walked on. 'That's shaken me more than a little,' he told Ginger when they were out of earshot. 'Caught me on one foot, in fact. Joudrier was quite definite that Marcel's machine wasn't on the airfield, and I took his word for it. Moreover, I'm sure the machine wasn't here yesterday. I walked past that hangar. The Vietnam Douglas wasn't there then, so had the Morane been there I would have been bound to spot it.'

'You've no doubt about it being Marcel's machine?'

'None, whatever. The behaviour of those mechanics proves there's something phoney about it. They wouldn't have kicked up that fuss had they not been given orders to keep people out. Actually, there's been no real reason why we should be astonished at finding the Morane. We know it came here, and provided it was still airworthy, what more likely place to find it than the airfield?'

'Even if it is Marcel's machine, that's about all it tells us,' said Ginger gloomily.

'On the contrary it tells us a lot,' disputed Biggles. 'It has given us some good news. It's the first ray of hope we've had that Marcel is still alive. The machine is airworthy. It was in the air this morning – or at any rate the engine was run up. It wasn't crashed, either by accident or design, so if Marcel is dead he didn't die that way; and if he wasn't killed in a crash there must be a chance that he's still alive. Moreover, if he's still alive, as the 'plane is here he can't be far away. That's how it looks to me. I may be taking an optimistic view, but the fact that we've found the machine has cheered me a lot. By hook or by crook we must find out who's using the machine now.'

'If you walk about asking questions you may start something.'

'It can't be avoided. No one's likely to tell us if we don't ask.'

'I have a feeling, judging by the behaviour of those two erks, that no one's likely to tell us if we *do* ask.'

'We shall see.'

'Where are you going to begin?'

'Here, at the airport; where else? Somebody must know what we want to know.'

Reaching the main hall Biggles went to a porter.

'There's a little machine, a Morane, in one of the hangars; do you happen to know if it's for sale or hire?'

The man gave Biggles a searching stare, while on his face dawned a faint suspicion of alarm. 'No,' he answered shortly.

'Well, can you tell me who it belongs to?'

The man's lips came together. 'I know nothing about 'planes,' he said, and turned his back.

Biggles walked over to a man in uniform, who looked as if he might be an assistant manager. 'Monsieur,' he said politely, 'my friend and I are having an argument which you may be able to settle for us.'

'*Oui, monsieur?*' answered the man pleasantly.

'In walking past the hangars we noticed a small 'plane painted green and brown and carrying a Chinese mark. My friend says it's a Breqnet. I say it's a Morane. Am I right?'

Long before Biggles had finished speaking the man's manner had changed. 'I know of no such aeroplane,' he answered curtly.

'But aren't you something to do with the traffic?'

'I am.'

'Do machines come and go without you knowing?'

'Sometimes.'

Mild sarcasm crept into Biggles' voice. 'You mean, people can fly in and park their planes anywhere, without reference to you?'

The man shrugged. 'Excuse me, I am busy.' He turned on his heels and walked away.

'A poor liar,' was Biggles' opinion of him. 'No matter. We have at least learned this much. Behind whatever is going on here is someone powerful enough to scare these people into keeping their mouths shut. The one thing

T—B

that does stick out a mile is, asking questions here isn't going to get us anywhere.'

'It might – but not where we want to get,' returned Ginger meaningly.

'The alternative is to watch and see who takes the Morane out. As it has recently been out it's unlikely to to go out again today, so we might as well go back to the hotel for lunch and give the others the gen. We haven't done so badly for one morning.'

*

The remainder of the daylight hours passed without any incident to cast fresh light on the mystery of the Morane and the more serious matters involved. After lunch, during which Biggles gave Algy and Bertie the latest news, he and Ginger returned to the airport to watch the place generally and the shed housing the Morane in particular. The others, very bored, continued to play their parts as salesmen, for apart from the advisability of maintaining these roles there was really nothing else they could do.

With the coming of darkness, which put an end to outdoor observations, having spent a fruitless afternoon, Biggles and Ginger returned to the hotel, as, of course, did Algy and Bertie.

They were together in the lounge, quietly discussing the situation over a pot of tea, when a soft-footed Annamite waiter came in, walked up to the table and informed Biggles that Monsieur Estere, the manager, would like a word with him in his office, if he would be so kind as to step along.

Biggles, naturally, looked surprised. 'Are you sure he means me?'

'*Oui, monsieur*,' confirmed the waiter and retired.

Biggles looked at the others. 'Now what?' he breathed. 'What on earth could he want with me – unless. . . .' He got up. 'Wait here,' he told them, and getting up made his way to the manager's office – the door marked Private from which he had seen Bollard emerge.

A few seconds later he was looking at the hotel manager for the first time; and what he saw caused him to brace himself for an interview which he knew was going to be difficult, for he both disliked and distrusted the man on sight. But still, he reflected, the man no doubt knew his job well enough; for all over the world the Swiss enjoy a reputation in that capacity second to none.

Estere was typical of the type – medium build, good-looking in an unemotional sort of way, immaculate in his person and very well dressed. His face was pale, and at the moment entirely without expression; and it may be said here that throughout the interview it never changed. His face he could control, but not his eyes. Grey, and rather wide apart, in some queer way they reminded Biggles of those of an Alsatian dog watching a stranger. They were cold, suspicious and alert.

He did not invite Biggles to be seated. Instead, in a voice as expressionless as his face he began to speak. 'I understand you have spent the day at the airport?'

'Quite right.'

'And in one of the hangars you saw an aeroplane that excited your curiosity.'

'That's putting it strongly. Say I was interested.'

'Why?'

'If this is to be a game of quiz it's my turn. Is there any reason why, as a professional pilot, I shouldn't be interested in aeroplanes? And secondly, what has that to do with you?'

Estere ignored the questions. 'Why were you asking about that particular 'plane?'

Biggles bridled at this unwarranted interrogation, but he held himself in hand. 'There's no secret about it,' he said evenly. 'I merely wondered how a 'plane of that type got here, and who brought it. Is there anything wrong with that?'

'Nothing. But the fact remains, you were asking questions, and at Saigon at the present time that can be a dangerous occupation. As you are staying in my hotel I thought it my duty to warn you.'

'That was very considerate of you. At the moment you seem to be doing plenty of questioning. Tell me, Mr. Estere, why should it be more dangerous to ask questions here than anywhere else?'

'Because the war has brought many strange people here – some of them undesirable – and they resent interference. This place is full of spies of several nationalities, and when no man dare trust another nerves tend to become frayed and tempers short. Having a business to run I do my best to avoid trouble.'

'Quite so. I can understand that.'

'How long do you intend to stay here?'

'No longer than I can help, you may be sure. But that decision does not entirely rest with me. We shall leave, I imagine, as soon as the business that brought us here is concluded. Exactly how long that will be I can't say.'

'From the lack of success your employers are meeting it shouldn't be long. That's really all I wanted to say.'

What prompted Biggles to pursue the matter on the lines he did after what was obviously a dismissal, he

himself may not have known. It may have been sheer
devilment. It may have been resentment at the interrogation and the almost rude way in which it had been
conducted; an interrogation which, as he knew perfectly
well, had been intended to convey a hint that he and his
party were included in the undesirables to whom Estere
had alluded. Or it may have been a desire to retaliate,
to hit back. Estere had gone out of his way to give him
something to think about. Now he would give the suave
manager something to occupy *his* mind.

'It's curious that you should ask me to come and see
you,' he said smoothly, 'because, before leaving, I had
intended to come to see you.'

'With what object?'

'On the advice of a man I believe you know; an
American named Bollard.'

'What of him?'

'Last night, having perhaps taken a little too much to
drink, he told me – speaking as one airman to another –
that on his job he was able to what he called make a few
dollars on the side. He was thinking no doubt, that I
should soon be returning to Europe with a lightly loaded
aircraft. Naturally, as times are hard, I asked him how
he did it.'

'Did he tell you?'

'No. He wouldn't say. But he promised to give me an
introduction to you on his return – if I was still here.'

It was some seconds before Estere answered, and
Biggles knew his shot had gone home.

'What exactly do you mean by that?' asked the
manager, speaking distinctly.

'I was going to ask you what *you* thought Bollard
meant by it.' Biggles was smiling faintly.

Estere did not smile. The lids of his eyes dropped a fraction, so that they looked more than ever like those of an Alsatian. Speaking with slow deliberation he said: 'Are you trying to be funny at my expense?'

'My dear sir,' answered Biggles curtly, 'if you think I have come all this way to engage in an enterprise so unprofitable, you flatter yourself.'

'Is it then that you are trying to be clever?'

'Possibly. After all, most of us try to be that.'

'There is such a thing as being too clever. It often leads those who practise it into trouble – serious trouble.'

'That sounds almost like a threat.'

'I am giving you my advice. You are not in London, you know. This is Saigon, a town where wise men mind their own business.'

'That is precisely what I'm doing.'

'And what exactly is your business?'

'The same as yours. Earning my living.'

'You seem to go the hard way about it.'

'We can't all get in the easy money.'

'Why did you mention Bollard's name to me?'

'Because he mentioned you to me. Until then I didn't even know your name.'

'What did he tell you?'

'He told me nothing except what I've told you. Rightly or wrongly I gathered you helped him to augment his salary. If I'm wrong, forget it. I couldn't care less. Bear in mind I didn't ask to see you. You wanted to see me. Now we've seen each other. It doesn't seem to have got either of us very far, but there's still time.'

'As you say, there's still time.'

'If that's all I'll get along.'

'Think over what I've told you.'

'You might think over what I've told *you*.'

Biggles was turning to leave the room when there came an urgent rap on the door, which, without invitation, was thrown open, and a Chinese, dressed in European clothes, hurried into the room. In his hands he carried a newspaper. This, half-folded, he put on Estere's desk, and saying something quickly in a language Biggles did not understand, pointed at a picture.

Biggles' eyes, of course, went to it, but as from his position in front of the desk the reproduction was upside-down he could only see that it was a portrait. The paper, he noted, was the *Saigon-Soir*.

Estere, as if he realized suddenly that Biggles was still there, looked up. 'Good night,' he said shortly. 'I'll speak to you again some other time.'

'Good night, and thanks for the advice,' Biggles replied and left the room.

In a couple of minutes he had rejoined the others. 'Listen,' he said tersely. 'Things are beginning to warm up. It was asking questions about the Morane this morning that did it. The news wasn't long reaching Estere. Not that we need be surprised at that.'

'What about it, old boy, what about it?' demanded Bertie.

'Estere as good as gave me orders to get out.'

'Out of his beastly hotel?'

'And out of Saigon.'

'He's got a nerve,' muttered Algy.

'I'd say he's got very good nerves, and, unless we're right off track, he needs them for the game he's playing. He's suspicious of us. Nothing more than that, yet, I think; because if he knew definitely what we were doing he wouldn't have troubled to give us a warning. In a way he told me more than I told him. In sending for me he has as good as told us that he's in the big racket that's going on here. But make no mistake. From now on we're marked men; which means that we shall have to step warily or we shall end up like Marcel – however that may be. Incidentally, just as I was leaving a chap came in with a newspaper. He seemed to be a bit rattled. It was the *Saigon-Soir*. Ginger, you might slip out and get a copy. Make it snappy.'

Ginger departed.

'Have you any idea of what was in the paper to cause the flap?' asked Algy.

'None whatever. It may have something to do with our business; but there's a picture on the front page that's evidently of importance to Estere, and if it's of importance to him it may mean something to us.'

Ginger returned, carrying the paper folded across the middle. He handed it to Biggles, who opened it as he had seen it on Estere's desk, showing the picture. He glanced at it. The glance became a stare; a stare of incredulity. They all stared. No one spoke.

The picture was a head and shoulders photograph of a man wearing an open-necked shirt. The face was thin, haggard and unshaven. Below was the caption. In heavy type it announced: DANGEROUS MURDERER WANTED BY THE POLICE. Small italics gave the information that the man was a renegade who had been fighting with the Viet-Minh rebels. He had been captured and brought to Saigon, but had escaped during the night.

Ill and hollow-eyed though the face was, there was no mistaking it. The man was Marcel Brissac.

Biggles drew a breath sharply. 'That's what we wanted to know. This is where we get cracking. We haven't a minute to waste, because if they get him now he's had it. Estere, or the man behind it, will see to that.'

'Hadn't we better send a cable to Joudrier?' suggested Ginger anxiously.

'There's no time for that. With everyone on the watch, and in view of the state he's in, it can only be a matter of hours before they get him. And once they get him it won't take them long to silence him, because quite obviously, he knows too much.'

'If he only knew we were here,' muttered Ginger.

'Ifs won't get us anywhere. We've got to think hard and fast.'

'But where are we going to start looking for him in this rabbit warren of a town?' said Algy, a rising in-flection in his voice. 'He may not be in the town. He may –'

'All right. Let's not get in a panic,' broke in Biggles. 'Let's use our heads. Put yourself in Marcel's place, a fugitive in a now hostile town. Where would you make for?'

'The jungle,' suggested Ginger.

'And die of hunger or malaria – if you weren't stabbed to death by the rebels? I can't believe you'd be such a fool as that. Personally, I'd make for the airport. So, I fancy, will Marcel. He's got a machine there, don't forget. Even if he can't get to it he might grab another. In a matter of life or death he won't be particular. He's no hope of getting out of this country any other way than by air, and he must know it.'

'So you suggest we go to the airport,' said Ginger eagerly.

'Can you think of any other possibility?'

'No.'

'Anyone else any ideas?'

No one answered.

'Very well,' said Biggles. 'The airport it is. We'll split up and patrol the boundary road, concentrating on the stretch nearest the hangars. We needn't bother about the airport buildings. For obvious reasons he'll keep clear of them. We might call his name occasionally, or sing snatches of R.A.F. songs. The locals will hardly be likely to recognize them but Marcel might.'

'When do we start?' asked Algy.

'Now.'

'It's as black as pitch outside and pouring with rain,' put in Ginger.

'So much the better. It should give Marcel a chance.'

'And how long do we keep this up?'

'All night. In fact, till we find him, or hear he's been recaptured. Should that happen – but we'll talk of that when the time comes. The rendezvous is behind the hangar in which the Halifax is parked. I'll take that particular beat. Let's go.'

'Just a minute, old boy,' requested Bertie. 'What about this stinker Estere? His gang will be on the job, too.'

'What of it?'

'What's he going to think when we don't come home to roost?'

'I don't care two hoots what he thinks,' answered Biggles, in a tone of voice that settled any argument on that score.

Putting on their mackintoshes in the hall they walked towards the door.

Estere appeared. 'Going out?' he inquired.

'Do you mind?' asked Biggles, with biting sarcasm.

'Not at all. It's raining heavily.'

'We've been out in the rain before,' Biggles told him.

'Would you like me to call you a taxi?'

'No thanks. If you're so anxious to know where we're going I'll tell you. For something to do we've decided to make a round of these famous Saigon night clubs we've heard about.'

'Be careful.'

'Of what?'

'You may have your pockets picked.'

Biggles smiled. 'What a man you are for warnings! Your nerves must be as shaky as those of the people you were telling me about. It must be something in the atmosphere of Saigon, or the sort of life you lead. Good night.'

They slushed up the dripping pavement for some distance before Biggles hailed a taxi and told the driver to take them to the airport.

*

For the task on hand the night could hardly have been worse. The atmosphere was oppressive, with an element of unreality, and as dark as only a moonless tropic night can be. Except for an occasional interval the rain fell in a steady downpour. The pot-holes in the road, which had been cut to pieces by heavy military traffic, became deep puddles from which, when the rain ceased, mosquitoes rose in swarms. Air and earth seemed to be turning to water, and Ginger, peering into the darkness, soon gave up trying to keep dry.

It was one of the longest nights he could remember.

The darkness did, in fact, last for nearly twelve hours. He thought it would never end. The monotony of his occupation no doubt made it seem worse. He would walk a little way, splashing through the mire, call Marcel's name, listen, and then blunder on until he met Bertie, who had the next beat. After a few words he would turn about and repeat the performance until he met Algy, who was his other contact man. Of all the futile vigils he had ever undertaken this seemed to be the most hopeless, but with Marcel's life at stake, and no alternative, it had to be done.

Once in a while he encountered another pedestrian of the night. Who or what he might be he never knew, for no greetings were exchanged. A vague figure would emerge from the gloom, steer a cautious course on the far side of the steaming road, and disappear again in the murk. Once a convoy of trucks went past, their headlights blurred, the vehicles filled with the huddled figures of troops returning from the front or from some sinister operation. Once, too, he had an anxious moment when a jeep came along. It stopped. A man jumped down and flashed a torch in his face. Recognizing the uniform of the military police, Ginger pretended to be drunk.

'Who are you and what are you doing here?' asked the man.

'My answer to both questions is, I don't know and I don't care,' answered Ginger thickly.

The man laughed, as did others in the car; and Ginger breathed a sigh of relief when it went on, his ruse apparently succeeding. The thought occurred to him that these men might also be looking for Marcel.

Throughout the whole miserable ordeal he was fortified by his anxiety, and pity, for Marcel, whose plight must be much worse than his own. But his dominant sensation was one of mounting disappointment, for he had started off in high hopes, inspired by the knowledge that Marcel was still alive and might well make for the airfield; but as the weary hours dragged on his spirits began to hang as heavily as his saturated clothes. Anger, and hatred for the people responsible for it all, took root.

Dawn, dreary and water-logged, found them all together behind the hangar that housed the aircraft.

'I'm going to keep on,' stated Biggles grimly. 'We'll stay here all day and again tonight if necessary. I can't think of anywhere else Marcel would be likely to go.'

'Why doesn't he go to police headquarters?' said Algy. 'After all, Marcel is a policeman, so you'd think he'd get in touch with the authorities here. That aspect has struck me all along as queer.'

'There's obviously some reason why he can't, or hasn't done that,' replied Biggles. 'In some way it must be tied up with that picture in the paper, which was either issued by the police or made to look like that. I suspect the truth is this. Conditions here are much like they were in America when the country was practically run by gangsters, and nobody dare speak for fear of being bumped off. Marcel daren't be seen and he daren't trust a soul. His only hope of breaking the thing up is to get out of the country; and his only hope of getting out is to fly out. That's why I gambled on him coming here. The danger is, other people will work that out, and they'll be along. If they see us here they'll guess what we're doing.'

'We shall also know what they're doing,' put in Bertie warmly, 'and if they start any bumping tricks we can bump with the best of 'em, yes, by Jove!'

'If things are as bad as they appear to be, I doubt if Marcel will dare to move in daylight,' opined Algy.

'He could move without necessarily showing himself,' Biggles pointed out. 'There's plenty of cover. He could work his way along this ditch, or through the scrub, to get to the hangars.' He indicated the two obstacles that separated the road from the landing area. 'All right,' he concluded. 'You carry on as you were. I'll join you presently. Under the pretext of doing a top overhaul I'm going to get the Halifax out in case we should need it in a hurry.'

'If you move the machine Estere will be told,' warned Ginger.

'I can't help that. He may think I've taken his advice and am getting ready to pull out.'

'Don't you think you ought to send Joudrier a cable?' said Algy.

'The contents of any cable I send from here will be in Estere's hands inside half an hour,' answered Biggles succinctly, 'and, moreover, if we break the party up by sending someone into the town, we may never get together again; in which case instead of one man being missing there might be two or three. But that's enough talking. Get back on your beats but not too far apart. It's only necessary to cover the ground behind the hangars. They'll be Marcel's objective if he comes this way.'

The party broke up, Biggles pushing through the scrub and taking a short cut to their hangar, and the others lining the road at intervals of about fifty yards. It was no longer raining. The cloud layer seemed to be lifting, with the result that visibility was steadily improving. This, as Ginger realized, cut two ways. It was

an advantage in that it gave them a better chance of
seeing Marcel if he was about; but that would also
apply to Marcel's enemies. Marcel would realize that,
and if he moved at all it would be under cover.

The thought that occurred constantly to Ginger as he
paced up and down was, if only Marcel knew they were
there – or even in Saigon. Their chances of getting together would at once be tremendously improved. But
on the face of it there was no possible way of bringing
about this desirable state of affairs.

Suddenly he stopped dead in his tracks. Another
minute and he had jumped the ditch, pushed his way
through the scrub, and was racing across the soaking
turf to where the Halifax, its engines muttering, was
turning slowly head to wind on the concrete apron.
Biggles was in the cockpit. Ginger beckoned frantically.
Biggles jumped down. 'What's happened?'

'Nothing's happened, but I've got an idea.'

'Shoot.'

'If the Halifax was in the air it could be seen for miles
around. Marcel would see it and recognize it. He'd
know that no one but us would be likely to bring a
Halifax here. Think what that would mean! Wherever
he is and whatever he's doing it would bring him to the
airfield hot foot.'

'Great work. Full marks,' snapped Biggles. 'Why
didn't we think of it before? I'll take the machine off
right away, ostensibly for a test, and fly first round the
perimeter and then over the town. Warn the others
what I'm doing. I'll fly low over you occasionally. If you
want me to come in hold your arms out level.'

'Okay.' With the roar of the Halifax's engines in his
ears Ginger hurried back to the road and told Algy and

Bertie the latest plan. Then, with new hope in his heart, he returned to his beat and took up a position on a bank that gave a fair view of the surrounding country. Overhead the Halifax was cruising low round the aerodrome boundary.

Presently a jeep came along. There were two uniformed men in it. Their caps were red. From time to time the man next to the driver stood up and looked around, and Ginger did not need to be told the purpose of this procedure. Nor was he surprised when, the car drawing level, the standing man called to him. 'Have you seen a villainous-looking fellow who walks with a limp?'

'I have seen only some coolies working in the paddy fields,' answered Ginger truthfully.

'What are you doing, standing there?'

'I'm watching that big 'plane fly round.'

The two men had a brief discussion, and from the way they looked at him Ginger knew he was the subject of it. Then to his great relief the car drove on. He watched it with apprehension, for if it was going to patrol the road it was not likely to make their task any easier. The police were looking for a man with a limp. If, as he supposed, it was Marcel they were looking for, then he had evidently suffered some injury. Still watching the car he saw it stop when it reached Algy, who was walking down the road. Words were exchanged. The vehicle went on a little way, turned, came back, and passing Ginger without stopping continued on to the airport buildings. The two men got out and were joined by a number of others standing there.

It was now plain to Ginger that he, that all of them, were being watched. It was equally plain that the present state of affairs would not be allowed to go on much longer. What would happen he didn't know and couldn't guess, but that an end would be made to what they were doing he was sure.

The clatter of a single-engined aircraft being started up made him turn to the airfield. For a moment or two a hangar covered his view; then the Morane came into sight, taxi-ing. For a wild instant he thought it might be Marcel getting away; but this hope was soon squashed. The machine did not even take off, but taxied on to the front of the booking hall, where it stopped and the engine died. Ginger smiled mirthlessly when he realized that this was merely a precaution to prevent anyone from approaching the aircraft without being seen. At least, that was what he supposed.

Still watching, he noticed an unusual amount of activity outside the main entrance. Walking a little nearer he thought he could make out the well-dressed Esterc talking to a Chinese, also well-dressed, and some police – or soldiers, he wasn't sure which. At any moment now, he knew, trouble would arrive.

The Halifax passed over very low, as if Biggles had decided to come in. Was that, Ginger wondered, what the police were waiting for? Did they, on some trumped up charge, intend to seize the machine? Obviously that could happen, and if it did the position would be grim indeed. He hurried to a nearby unmanned concrete gun emplacement and climbed on it for a better view, to watch if the Halifax did actually land. From the top he snatched a glance in the direction of Algy to see what he was doing, feeling that it was time they got together for mutual help should trouble arise. Apparently Algy was thinking on the same lines, for he was beckoning to Bertie who was farther along.

Satisfied, Ginger was turning away when a movement caught his eye. It was only a fleeting glimpse, but he distinctly saw a crouching figure cross a sparse area of scrub, on the airfield side of the road, about fifty yards from where he stood. In a flash he had slid off the pill-box and was running towards the spot, also crouching low to avoid being seen from the airport buildings. As he drew near he shouted 'Marcel'.

A faint voice answered.

Ginger plunged into the bushes, and there on his knees was Marcel, although in such a dreadful state was he that for a moment he was not sure of it. He was in rags, mired from head to foot. There were jungle sores on his face and a blood-stained bandage showing through a long rent in his trouser leg. He was breathing heavily and was obviously at his last gasp.

Ginger could have wept with compassion. 'Okay, Marcel,' he said huskily. 'Hang on. We're all here. Just a minute.' He dashed back to the road to call up Algy and Bertie; but they must have seen him running, and guessing something was afoot were coming at the double. 'Come on!' he cried urgently. 'He's here! But he's in a bad way and we may have to carry him.' He ran back to Marcel, and the others arrived a moment later.

'We've no time to lose,' rapped out Ginger. 'We were being watched. They'll come to see what we're doing.'

'Stand fast while I see where Biggles is,' answered Algy crisply, and forced a passage through the scrub for sight of the landing ground. Within a minute he was back. 'He's coming in towards the hangar,' he announced. 'Dash out, Ginger, and tell him to get as close as he can. I'm afraid Marcel's passed out and it means carrying him.'

Ginger started off, but stopped when he heard the jeep racing up the road. 'Here they come,' he panted.

The men in the jeep must have marked well the spot where Ginger had disappeared; but they may not have known that Algy and Bertie had joined him. The jeep stopped, and the same two men who had accosted him came bursting through the bushes.

It was no time for explanations, and before the red-caps could draw their pistols from the holsters on their belts Algy and Bertie had flung themselves on them. All four went down in a heap.

The struggle that followed was furious but short. The men, who may not have been genuine police, but were in any case in the pay of the racketeers, must have been astonished by the violence of the attack made on them and were at a disadvantage from the outset. Actually, they looked thoroughly scared and did not put up much of a fight. Ginger, whose temper had been brought to the boil by the appalling condition in which he had found Marcel, went into action like a fury, with the result that the two men, before they could have had time to grasp what was happening, were being held down on their backs by hands that were none too gentle.

'Tie 'em up,' rasped Algy. 'It's neck or nothing now.'

The arms of the prisoners were pinioned with their own belts. They were relieved of their pistols. 'We may need those,' said Algy, with iron in his voice. 'Come on. Get hold of Marcel. We shall have to carry him.'

'We shall be spotted the moment we leave the bushes,' Bertie pointed out.

'So what? We can't stay here.'

'Just a minute,' put in Ginger. 'What about the jeep?'

'What about it?'

'Why not load Marcel in it and drive in?'

'How are we going to get it across the ditch?'

'Let's drive in through the gate this side of the booking hall. It's always open.'

'They'll spot us.'

'They'll give way when they see we have no intention of stopping. If we borrow those red kepis they won't realize it's us until we're through.'

'Ginger's right,' declared Bertie. 'Absolutely. It would take us ten minutes to carry Marcel to the machine and they'd be on us like a ton of bricks.'

'Okay,' agreed Algy. 'Get the jeep turned round, Ginger. We'll bring Marcel.'

Ginger ran to the vehicle, and after two shunts, in which he nearly ditched it, had it facing the right direction. By that time Algy and Bertie appeared, half carrying, half dragging Marcel's limp body, which was arranged as comfortably as possible in the cramped space. 'All right. Let her go,' ordered Algy. 'Don't stop for anything. This is it.'

The gears engaged and the jeep moved forward, gathering speed.

By the time it had reached the gate by the main building it was doing forty; but faced with a right-angled turn, and knowing the tendency of a jeep to overturn when cornering at high speed, Ginger had to steady the pace; but he was still going fast when he shot through the gates. He had a glimpse of the startled faces of the men who had held out their arms to stop him, then he was through. Some shots were fired but none touched him.

His objective now was the Halifax, from which, having reached the tarmac, Biggles was just descending. Biggles stopped, staring, when he saw the approaching vehicle.

'Throw those hats away – he'll think we're police!' Ginger flung the words over his shoulder.

The hats which had served their purpose went overboard, and from the way Biggles moved Ginger saw that he had recognized them. He brought the jeep to a skidding stop. 'We've got him,' he yelled.

'Can you manage?'

'Yes! Get to the stick! Look out, they're coming!'

A number of men, strung out, were racing towards the machine; but they had too much ground to cover, and the nearest was still some distance away when, with Marcel inside, Ginger slammed the door. 'All clear,' he yelled.

The Halifax's engines bellowed. Ginger sank down. 'Phew!' he gasped. 'What a do.'

When wheel vibration ceased, telling him they were airborne, he scrambled to a side window and saw faces, upturned, sweeping past below. Turning to where Algy and Bertie, the first-aid chest on the floor beside them, were already at work on Marcel, he asked, anxiously, 'How is he?'

Algy answered. 'Nothing serious, I think. Exposure and exhaustion mostly, I imagine. He hung on till he saw us and then collapsed.'

Ginger went forward to the cockpit and passed the information on to Biggles. He told him briefly what had happened on the ground. 'Where are we making for?' he inquired.

'Rangoon for a start. Then flat out for Marseilles. I'm hoping to beat Bollard to it. He said he didn't hurry. Get one of the others to work out a course for me as soon as Marcel is comfortable.'

'Can't I do it?'

'No. You get in the tail and watch for a machine

following us. That gang is good enough for anything and may still try to stop us. If you see another machine, warn me, and I'll dodge into the overcast.'

'Okay. It's a bit of a bind having to abandon our kit.'

'I'll cable the British Legation from Rangoon and ask them to collect and forward it. For a little while it looked as if we might leave more behind than our small-kit.'

'Are you telling me!' muttered Ginger, and went aft.

*

Five days later the Halifax touched down at Marginane, the big airport of Marseilles. Bollard had not arrived, but Captain Joudrier of the Sûreté was there, in response to a signal sent by Biggles from Rome.

By this time Marcel was on his feet, although he was still shaky. His story was a simple one. From the start he had suspected the Ching Loo organization of being the worst offenders in the currency racket, because their profits, as he had ascertained in Paris, were out of proportion with their legitimate business. Which was why he had gone to the Pagoda Palace. There, he thought, he must have been recognized, for without warning he was seized and taken to Ching Loo's country house for questioning. He had in fact been tortured. By pretending to be unconscious he had managed to escape and had fled into the jungle. While seeking food he had been captured by the rebels, and by pretending to be in sympathy with them had lived with them for a while. The end of this came when the village in which he was hiding was captured by French government troops, who took him to Saigon. Unaware of the ramifications of the Ching Loo gang, he had, naturally enough, revealed his identity, expecting to be released. Instead of which he was accused of being a renegade and thrown into a punishment compound to await trial. Knowing what his fate would be when Ching Loo learned of this, he had again escaped, on this occasion being wounded in the thigh by a bullet. Hiding in a paddy field, he had, as was hoped, seen the Halifax, and realizing what this meant had made a desperate attempt to reach the airfield. Of the seizure of his own aircraft he knew nothing. The Ching Loo people had presumably taken it over for their own use. They needed aircraft for making contact with the rebels, with whom they were trading, an unsuspected piece of evidence that Marcel had discovered while he was with them. Of Bollard he knew nothing.

Bollard arrived on the aerodrome on the following day, by which time plans had been made for his reception. Only he and his partner got out of the Douglas, which was kept under observation. Carrying the portfolio and attaché-case he was allowed to pass through the barrier into the booking hall, where Biggles was waiting for him, the others watching from a distance. His astonishment at seeing Biggles was genuine, as was, no doubt, his greeting: 'What the heck are you doing here?'

'I came along to meet you,' answered Biggles. 'Let's go over here and sit down.'

'What's the big idea?' demanded Bollard, when they reached the seat.

'Simply this,' replied Biggles. 'You're on a spot, and I'd advise you in all seriousness to come clean.'

'I don't get it,' declared Bollard

'You will,' Biggles promised. 'Tell me, what have you got in that portfolio?'

'Papers.'

'What sort of papers?'

'How would I know? He said business papers.'

'Who said – Estere?'

Bollard hesitated. 'Yes.'

'Haven't you looked in the bag?'

'No. I can't. It's locked, I took his word for it.'

'You weren't given a key!'

'No.'

'What were you to do with the case?'

'Hand it over to Ching Loo's manager at the company's office in Marseilles.'

'Suppose we have a look inside?'

'Not on your life.'

Biggles shook his head. 'It's no use, Bollard. The Customs people have every right to search you, you know that.' He beckoned to Joudrier and the uniformed men with him.

Bollard went pale when he saw them. 'Okay,' he said helplessly. 'But if these papers are confidential there may be trouble.'

'What did Estere pay you for carrying the bag?'

'Fifty bucks.'

'And you take another bag back to Saigon when you go?'

'Sure.'

'And is that how you made your money on the side?'

'Yep. What's wrong with that? Estere wanted the papers home fast and I was coming with an empty crate.'

'What about the passenger you picked up at Saigon?'

That shook Bollard. For a moment he was speechless. 'So you know about that!'

Biggles nodded. 'We were watching. Who was he?'

Bollard smiled wryly. 'He didn't pay anything for the

lift. He was just a Yank who wanted to get home.'

'A deserter?'

'Sure.'

'Where is he now?'

'I dunno. I dropped him off in Rome. He said he could manage from there. He would rather not step out on French territory.'

'I thought it might be something like that,' murmured Biggles.

All eyes were now on Joudrier, who had taken the portfolio and was trying a succession of keys in the lock. Suddenly it flew open. Without a word he showed the contents. It was packed with bundles of bank-notes.

Bollard took it surprisingly calmly. 'Okay. I'm the sucker,' he said quietly. 'What do you want me to do?'

'Deliver this to the address as arranged,' answered Joudrier. 'We shan't be far away.'

*

That, as far as Biggles and his friends were concerned, was really the end of the Saigon adventure. They went straight on home, leaving the French police to clean up the business in their own way. This they did with their usual realistic thoroughness, a special force of police being flown from Paris to Saigon to make sure there was no mistake.

Today, the Ching Loo organization no longer exists. Estere is serving a long sentence in a French prison. Bollard, angry at the deception played on him, took sides with the police, and got away with a nominal fine. He lost his job, as was inevitable, but that didn't worry him overmuch. There were, he told Marcel, other 'planes, and better places than Saigon.

2

THE CASE OF THE MODERN PIRATE

BIGGLES and his police pilots looked up from some illustrations of a new type of aircraft in the current issue of *Flight* as the door of the Ops Room opened and their chief, Air Commodore Raymond, walked in.

'Happy New Year to you all,' he greeted cheerfully.

'Same to you, sir,' came back voices in unison.

'Have you come here merely to offer seasonal felicitations?' inquired Biggles suspiciously.

'No,' answered the Air Commodore, frankly.

'That's what I thought,' murmured Biggles.

'I have come,' went on the Air Commodore, as he dropped into a chair, 'to tell you a story which supports my oft-repeated statement that modern crime, in actual fact, is streets ahead of imaginative fiction.'

'I'm ready to believe anything,' asserted Biggles.

'Don't be too sure,' warned the Air Commodore, the corners of his mouth twitching as if he were slightly amused. 'What a thief lifted on one occassion was no trifle that could be slipped into the pocket, or even thrown into the back of a car. The object weighed several thousand tons.'

Even Biggles looked a bit taken aback. Then a slow smile spread over his face. 'I see what you mean about imagination,' he agreed. 'What was this object?'

'A steamship.'

'You mean a launch.'

'I mean a three thousand ton, deep sea job, new off the stocks.'

Biggles' smile broadened. 'That *is* something,' he conceded. 'From shop-lifting to ship-lifting is quite a step. What did this smart lad do with the swag?'

'He lost it.'

'Where?'

'That's what we want to know.'

Biggles sighed. 'Ah! I get it. And this is where we start a little game of hunt the thimble round the globe.'

'That's the general idea; but it isn't quite as bad as that.'

'There is this about a ship, old boy,' put in Bertie. 'The bally thing is big enough to see. I mean to say, it isn't the sort of thing you could drop somewhere without somebody stumbling over it.'

'Yes. You've got something there,' allowed Biggles, sarcastically. He looked at the Air Commodore. 'Give us the gen about this astonishing effort. It promises to have the merit of being amusing.'

'The plot was certainly ingenious.'

'I presume the bloke wanted the ship for a particular purpose.'

'He wanted to be a pirate.'

Biggles laughed aloud. 'That's delicious. No doubt a lot of fellows would rather steer a ship on the briny than push a pen in an office, but it would take an uncommon amount of nerve today to hoist the Jolly Roger. Who was this modern Morgan?'

'His name is John Sebastian Blake. I use the present tense because, for all we know to the contrary, he's still alive. It seems that when he was a boy he read a book about pirates, and forthwith determined to be one. It's evident now that in this ambition he never wavered, although he said little about it. There was no need for him to do what he did because he was reasonably well off; so we can only conclude that he was urged by misguided romantic devilment to commit an act of folly for which he will have to pay – if he hasn't already paid with his life. But let me tell you the whole story in sequence. I must say it takes a bit of believing.' The Air Commodore accepted a cigarette from Biggles and continued.

'Blake was born, and brought up, on the coast of Devon. He loved the sea and was never far away from it. His one recreation was messing about with boats, and by the time he was in his teens he was a clever and fearless sailor. At school he was a brilliant pupil. An only son, his people doted on him, and no objection was raised when, on leaving school, he announced his wish to go to sea. That was only to be expected. He entered the mercantile marine as an apprentice and passed his examinations with a facility that must have been the result of natural ability combined with enthusiasm. So, for eight years, all went well. Whether all this time he was plotting the scheme he later put into practice, or whether it came in a flash of foolish inspiration, we don't know. But there was this about it. He knew all there was to know about ships, ships' papers and the like. For that very reason he should have known that his scheme was doomed to failure from the outset. Sooner or later, people wiser than he would be bound to catch up with him. Be that as it may, when he was twenty-six his father died and left him twelve thousand pounds. It was, presumably, for this money that he was waiting, in order to go "a-pirating" in what we may call a modern style.' The Air Commodore tapped the ash from his cigarette and continued.

'I must tell you here that Blake had taken at least one man into his confidence – probably several. This fellow was an American sailor with a bad record, although whether or not Blake was aware of his real character we don't know. Nor do we know where Blake first met him. It may have been in some foreign port. All that matters to us is, this man, Nicolas Diaz, was, from the start, in the conspiracy to steal a ship. The first moves were not difficult. Blake knew the ropes. With his £12,000 he opened an office as a ship-broker. He then advertised for a modern well-found ship for a special charter job lasting six months. This charter, he stated, was to enable a party of wealthy Americans to do a cruise starting from England. Money was no object. He was offered several ships, and the one he chose was named *Cygnet*. These Americans, he said, were bringing their own captain – and that, of course, is where Diaz came in. While Blake was attending to insurance, stocks of provisions, cargo, and so on, Diaz was collecting his crew. Most of them were coloured men, lascars and the like, who had served in P. and O. liners. The cargo included a lot of paint, for reasons which will presently become apparent. There was also a small printing press. Payment for all this stuff was only made in part. The balance would be forthcoming when the

Americans arrived. Naturally, the firms concerned didn't part with their goods without making inquiries; but as we know, Blake's company had £12,000 in the bank and that was considered good enough. In due course the *Cygnet* set sail.'

'What about these wealthy Americans who were supposed to be on board?' asked Biggles.

'Blake had provided for that by saying he was to pick them up at Lisbon; and as a matter of fact the *Cygnet* put in at Lisbon, its arrival being duly reported to the owners in London. The voyage was continued, ostensibly for Cape Town. Somewhere off the African coast Blake called his crew together, in the old pirate tradition, and told them what he intended to do. If they would join him in this adventure, he said, they would all get treble pay and a handsome bonus. To this attractive proposition all fell in line except two, one an Englishman named Farrow, and a Scotch engineer named Macalister. These two took no part in what followed. Diaz wanted to kill them, but Blake wouldn't have that. They were merely put in irons when the ship was in port. Incidentally, this seems to have been the first rift in the lute between Blake and Diaz. Other quarrels followed.'

'How did you learn these details?' inquired Biggles curiously.

'From Farrow, who was one of the few survivors of this fantastic adventure. But to continue. Passing near the reefs that make the coast of South-West Africa a mariner's nightmare when there's fog about, the *Cygnet* was stopped and a lot of gear thrown overboard – boats, lifebelts, and other stuff carrying the ship's name. The ship was painted black instead of grey, the white funnel became orange, and the name *Cygnet*, wherever it appeared, changed to *Pauline*. This included the ship's papers – hence the printing press. In a word, Blake, forgetting nothing, completely altered the identity of the ship. As the *Pauline* it went on to Cape Town where the cargo was sold for cash at cut prices. This put nearly £20,000 in Blake's pocket. Another cargo was taken aboard, without payment being made, this time ostensibly for South America. Clear of port the name *Pauline* was changed to *Corinthia*, and the ship went to Brisbane, Australia, where again the cargo was sold for cash. Get the idea?'

Biggles nodded. 'Sounds like money for old rope.'

'That's what Blake must have thought,' agreed the Air Commodore. 'By this time the faked wreckage of the *Cygnet*, the boats and so on, had been found, and the ship was written off as a dead loss. But there's an old saying, truth will out. Some of the cargo that had been sold in Cape Town found its way back to England. How did these goods get to Cape Town if the *Cygnet* was wrecked? The insurance companies got busy and the end of Blake's jaunt was in sight. They learned that the goods had been unloaded from a ship named *Pauline*. There was no such ship on Lloyd's Register. The description of the *Pauline* tallied with the *Cygnet*. Radio got busy, and every port in the world was warned to be on the look-out for the *Pauline*. By this time, as we know, there was no *Pauline*; but there was a vessel at Brisbane named *Corinthia* that looked mighty like her. She had just loaded a cargo, which included bar gold, for England. Radio flashed again, and it was learned that there was no ship of that class named *Corinthia*. Blake picked up these signals, and realizing that the game was up, slipped his cable during the night and headed north. Aircraft soon found her, and watched her until the monsoon, bringing rain, put an end to air observation. The rain was followed by a typhoon, and the *Corinthia*, undermanned and not daring to run to any port for shelter, was soon in a bad way. Trying to get into a creek along the coast of North-East Guinea a tidal wave threw her high and dry on the edge of a mangrove swamp. That was the pay-off. Blake, realizing the ship was finished, had the gold, the safe containing the money in notes, and the food stores, put off, and informing the crew that it was now every man for himself, gave every member five hundred pounds in notes – with injunctions to keep his mouth shut. Finally he set fire to the ship.

The crew, forming parties as it suited them, dispersed. Farrow and Macalister, who had refused to accept the silence money, managed to slip away, and from cover watched Blake and Diaz bury their ill-gotten gains which of course they couldn't carry with them.'

'Quite a story,' murmured Biggles. 'What was the end of all this?'

'That's a tale yet to be told,' averred the Air Commodore. 'None of these people could have had the remotest idea of what lay between them and Port Moresby, in Papua, on the far side of the island. That's where they decided to make for. Only recently was the island crossed for the first time, and then by a specially equipped expedition comprising two white men who knew the country, a large force of armed police and seventy-five bearers. And even they, able to get a certain amount of food on the way, had a thin time. As the crow flies the island is fifteen hundred miles long and four hundred wide. But a man can't travel as the crow flies. He is faced with crocodile-infested rivers, swamps, virgin jungle and warlike tribes of head-hunting cannibals. As if these obstacles were not enough, the spine of the country is a range of mountains up to sixteen thousand feet high and forty miles across. In short, it's just about one of the worst pieces of territory in the world.'

'I take it none of these pirates got through,' observed Biggles.

'That's quite the most extraordinary part of the story,' declared the Air Commodore. 'Farrow did get through, arriving in Port Moresby more dead than alive. He started with Macalister, who died of fever on the way. The fate of the rest remains a mystery, but as they haven't shown up anywhere it seems likely that they are all dead, and their heads now decorate some native village.'

'They must have had plenty of food available at the start.'

The Air Commodore shook his head. 'A man couldn't carry enough food to support himself on such a trip – not for the entire journey.'

'Then how did Farrow manage it?'

'Because by sheer luck he struck the head waters of the Fly River and had the nerve to steal a native canoe. Even then he wouldn't have made it had he not been found by a government inspection launch in the lower reaches.'

'And what's the position now?'

'The position is that somewhere along the two hundred mile stretch of coast between Karhar Island and Wewak there is the wreck of a ship, and buried within fifty yards of it, £200,000 in bar gold and nearly £100,000

T—C

in notes – that is, of course, assuming that Blake and Diaz haven't moved the stuff, which seems unlikely. The insurance people want the money and will pay ten per cent for its recovery. We want Blake and Diaz. Apart from that we shall have to check Farrow's story. After all, we've only his word for what happened.'

'Where is Farrow now?'

'Dead. He died the other day in the London Hospital for Tropical Diseases – presumably from some bug he picked up on his journey.'

'Pity. And that's all?'

'That's the lot. The job may turn out to be one for a land expedition; but it was thought that a lot of trouble might be saved if the wreck could be spotted by air reconnaissance. It's up your street and I wondered if you'd like to have a go at it. The main object is to ascertain if the gold is still there. If at the same time you could pick up any information about Blake or Diaz, so much the better.'

Biggles nodded. 'Fair enough. The trip would be a change from the usual routine. I'll think about it and let you know if the thing looks like a practical proposition. I believe there are two air companies now operating over New Guinea, so there shouldn't be any difficulty about fuel.'

'That's right. One company operates from Cooktown, in Australia, to Madang, via Port Moresby, and the other, if I remember, from Lae to Rabaul. Between these airfields, though, there is practically nothing but equatorial forest.'

'I'll go and have a look at the map,' concluded Biggles.

*

Nearly a month elapsed before the Air Police amphibian aircraft, Sea Otter, arrived at Madang, the base selected for the operation; for in view of the nature of the task the preparations had demanded exceptional care. Nothing could be left to chance; everything likely to be required, spare parts, provisions, weapons, and even trade goods to pacify hostile natives, had to be found, weighed, and stowed on board.

From his wide experience Biggles had a good idea of the difficulties most likely to confront them on the spot, and worked on the assumption that the job might well turn out to be a long one. As he more than once averred, the tragedy was that Farrow had died without revealing the position of the wreck. In the conditions in which the ship had been lost he may not have known the precise spot, but as a seaman he would at least have had a rough idea. In other words, had he been spared to accompany the expedition as a guide the enterprise would have been greatly simplified. But the man was dead, and they would have to manage without him.

From the maps that had been made available the party knew that the coast of North-East New Guinea was wild and rugged, but even so, it was not until a preliminary reconnaissance had been made that they appreciated fully the difficulties of the task they had undertaken. Ginger said frankly that he thought the business looked so hopeless that eventually it would have to be handed over to a ground force.

The territory was roughly two hundred miles in length; that is to say, that would have been the distance had the line been reasonably straight. But in actual fact the foreshore was so deeply indented that to follow it closely would mean a flight of nearer four hundred miles.

Again, the scene was remarkable in its variation, every kind of tropical coast being represented. There were places where the great mountains of the interior rolled right down to the sea. For mile after mile the vivid green of bamboo swamps alternated with the inevitable mangroves. From above, these looked harmless enough, but none of those in the aircraft needed to be told how different would be the picture presented from ground level; for if there is one place on earth where slime and beastliness have combined to breed creatures of horror, it is a tropic mangrove swamp.

Where the beach was sand it was mostly narrow and steeply shelving, so that convolvulus vines and other creepers, escaping from the forest, hung over it like a curtain. The formation of these beaches was peculiar. They consisted of a succession of tiny bays, with tongues of sand running out into the sea at frequent intervals, giving the impression that the water had bitten large mouthfuls out of the land. Skirting the coast were shallows and innumerable reefs. These were likely to prove a blessing, in that by breaking the waves that rolled in from the open sea they afforded plenty of anchorages. Islands, too, were common, lying like emeralds in water that varied in colour from turquoise to deepest ultramarine.

On this first trip the sky was as blue and cloudless as only a tropical sky can be, and as there was no wind the ocean lay smooth to a clean-cut horizon.

For five consecutive days the Otter cruised up and down the coast, Biggles determined to make the most of the fine weather, which he knew could change, in a few hours, to heavy rain. But for all that was seen the aircraft might as well have remained at its base, and even

Biggles was beginning to agree with Ginger that the job was hopeless. He flew high, he flew low, but it made no difference. From high altitudes the great equatorial forest could be seen rolling back mile after mile to the mighty mountain chain that forms the backbone of the island. Not once did the searchers see any sign of life, animal or human. But they were not deceived. They knew that under those same trees, engaged in constant warfare with each other, lived tribes of natives which, for sheer blood-lust, have no equal in the world. Civilization has only touched them by way of gold prospectors and missionaries, and they, more often that not, have left their heads to decorate some barbaric doorpost.

At the end of the fifth day Biggles announced that as they couldn't go on burning the petrol at the rate they were using it, he would send a signal to the Air Commodore advising him of the position. They would make one more flight, on the following day. If that yielded nothing he would call a halt until further instructions were received from London.

As it turned out, the sixth day proved to be the lucky one; at least, it was lucky as far as it provided the search party with their first clue. It came about this way.

Near the mouth of the Sepik River, on the fringe of the forest Ginger spotted a wisp of smoke. He called Biggles' attention to it and the aircraft went down to investigate. Ginger expected to see a party of natives, for as they lost height he made out a canoe pulled up on a beach clear of the water; but as Biggles glided low over the spot he was astonished by the sudden appearance of two white men, who ran out of the forest, waving frantically.

'As we can't speak to them from up here we'd better go down to see if those fellows are in trouble,' said Biggles, taking stock of the surface of the water, for the beach shelved too steeply for a landing. 'They may be able to tell us something,' he added.

After making a false run over the water to confirm that it was free from obstructions, he put the aircraft down without trouble, and churning a milky wake swung in to that part of the beach where the two men stood waiting. Stepping out into shallow, lukewarm water, the crew of the Otter waded ashore.

'Anything wrong?' greeted Biggles, although if appearances were not misleading the strangers were in poor shape. Both were thin, their clothes were in ribbons and they looked worn out. One was shaking with fever.

The men had a simple enough tale to tell. One was a New Zealander, the other Australian. They were gold prospectors, and had tried their luck up a tributary of the Sepik River. As usual there had been trouble with the natives, and they had been lucky to get away with their lives, having lost most of their provisions and equipment. For a month they had been working their way along the coast, trying to reach some point of contact with assistance. With food shortage and fever, and no quinine or mosquito nets, they were nearly at the end of their tether.

Biggles assured them that he could fix them up with food if they wished to continue on foot. Alternatively, he would give them a lift to Medang if that would suit them better.

They jumped at the offer of a passage that would take an hour instead of weeks of hard labour.

'A slice of luck for us you came along, chum,' said

the Australian, an ex-service man named Thompson. 'We couldn't believe our ears when we heard a plane. I suppose you weren't looking for us by any chance? We left word where we were going.'

'No,' answered Biggles. 'As a matter of fact we were looking for a wreck. Did you happen to see one as you came down the coast?'

'We must have seen half a dozen,' was the disconcerting reply. 'Most of 'em old. There was one, though, that we reckoned hadn't been there very long – biggish ship, she must have been, too.'

'The ship I'm looking for was mostly metal.'

'The sea would soon break her up,' declared Thompson. 'This is a bad bit of coast, although you might not think so looking at it today. If the sea didn't break her up the blacks would, bit by bit. They'd take the metal for spear and arrow heads.'

'Where was this?' inquired Biggles.

Thompson thought for a moment. 'Be about twenty miles west of here, on the far side of a sizeable creek. She was lying on the mud on the edge of a mangrove swamp. We spent a bit of time probing the mud with sticks hoping to strike some cans of grub, but there was nothing doing.'

'Sounds as if it might be what we're looking for,' said Biggles thoughtfully.

'If you're thinking of going that way you'd better watch your step,' declared Thompson. 'There's something going on and the blacks are in a nasty mood. They're Kobes. Usually they're not too bad, but something seems to have upset 'em. The V.C. told us a cock and bull story about them being attacked by Gilkiks – that's the next tribe – led by a white man with a rifle.

The two tribes are always at war. Anyhow, we found the atmosphere grim. We asked for grub, but all we got was threats. You can't trust these devils a yard. If it hadn't been for the V.C. I reckon we'd have gone into the cooking pot.'

'What's this V.C. you're talking about?'

'You must be new to these parts or you'd know. He's the Village Constable. A black, of course, usually a fellow who has been to Port Moresby and speaks a bit of pidgin English. Government pays him a pound or so a year to keep order. Some chap will usually take the job because he gets a uniform – a blue loin cloth edged with red. His badge of authority is a tin disc with the letters V.C. punched in it. The one in the Kobe village is scared rigid, because whichever side wins the war he's likely to be the meat in the sandwich.'

'You don't believe this tale about a white man leading the Gilkiks?'

'No. Who could he be? The only white man in the district is a well-known French priest belonging to the Sacre Coeur Mission, and he'd be the last man to carry a rifle, let alone start a war. We were hoping to see him but as soon as we mentioned his name, Father Antoinne, the blacks shut up like oysters; which means he's probably lost his head. That's what happens to most of these plucky padres at the finish. As I said just now, you can't trust these devils a yard. They'll beg medicine off you one day and slice off your head the next – for no reason at all.'

'I see,' said Biggles slowly. 'I find this all very interesting, but as it's too late to do anything today I'll run you down to Medang and come back tomorrow.'

'That suits us,' asserted the prospector. 'But watch

what you're doing or you'll find yourself in a stew – and when I say stew I mean stew. That Kobe country is no place for a white man right now.'

*

The fine weather held, and shortly after dawn the following day, the aircraft, flying low, was seeking the creek described by the prospectors. Below, the sea lay unruffled to the horizon. In the early morning light its colour was dove-grey, a strange and fascinating hue. There was as yet no play of tints or iridescence, or sparkle, as would come when the sun roused the day-wind.

Thompson had, overnight, presented Biggles with a rough sketch map, showing the position of the lost ship; yet even with this they were some time locating the spot, for creeks abounded, and all were much alike. It became evident that had it not been for the chance meeting with the prospectors, air reconnaissance on this occasion would have failed. Naturally, they had been looking for a wreck, and, moreover, the wreck of a fair-sized ship, and it was only when from ground level, they regarded all that was left of the ill-fated *Cygnet*, that they perceived clearly why they had failed to spot her. The hulk was beginning to show signs of listing, and its fire-ravaged funnel and plates were dull red with rust.

Without any means of identification Biggles was by no means convinced that this was the ship they sought, but as he averred, they could only work on the assumption that it was. At all events, the remains were those of a modern metal ship.

He took the Otter in as close as possible, for, as the tide was flowing, there was no risk of being left aground;

but, as there could be no question of using wheels on a
forshore of mud that was obviously soft, he left the
machine just afloat. The actual beach, strewn with the
debris of the island's vegetation, was forty or fifty yards
wide; but it would of course be less as the tide came in.
The wreck lay roughly in the middle. Behind rose the
wall of sinister-looking mangroves, black and menacing,
with surface roots that looped and arched like an army
of snakes. Under the dense foliage the swamp was a
place of shadows, of brooding silence, apparently devoid
of life, but, as Ginger knew from experience, was in fact
inhabited by loathsome creatures that could be either
fish or reptile. The air was hot and heavy with humidity.
From the evil-looking mud rose a stench of death and
decay.

Handing over the controls to Algy, with instructions
to be ready for a quick move, Biggles stepped out into a
foot of water and the same depth of mud. 'Not too bad,'
he announced. 'Ginger, you can come with me if you
like. Bertie, put some bullets in a gun and keep an eye
on us. If you see a movement anywhere, give us a hail,
but don't shoot unless things look serious.'

Followed by Ginger he floundered ashore, where the
mud, while slippery, had hardened somewhat. At the
same time, what Ginger had taken to be a log rose on
four legs and slithered into the water.

Biggles went on to the wreck. 'What a mess,' he
muttered, looking around.

'For any hope we've got of finding anything here we
might as well pack up and go home,' observed Ginger,
in a voice of disgust.

'I couldn't agree more,' answered Biggles, his eyes
roving the fringe of the mangroves. 'Probing the mud

single-handed we might be here for weeks without finding anything. Our only chance, as far as I can see, would be to get a squad of natives on the job.'

'What natives?' asked Ginger, looking startled.

'These Kobes, or whatever they're called, that Thompson told us about.'

'Hold hard,' protested Ginger. 'I'm all against ending up in an Irish stew.'

'They must have come here pretty often to carry away as much stuff as they have,' remarked Biggles, moving nearer to the mangroves. 'In which case,' he added, 'there should be a track of sorts leading to their village.'

'So what?' inquired Ginger cynically. 'Unless we're out of our minds the only track we shall take from here will be towards the Otter.'

'There *is* a track,' persisted Biggles. 'I can see it.'

Ginger could see it, too. And as his eyes followed it into the gloomy labyrinth he saw something else. A native, as rigid as the tree trunks themselves, was watching them. He could see only one. He was a tall, well-built man, with an unbelievably ugly face topped by a great mop of brushed-up hair. A small tusk was stuck through his nose and a string of teeth hung round his neck.

Recovering from his shock Ginger murmured: 'Don't move. We're being watched.'

'I can see him,' returned Biggles. 'Quite a lad, isn't he?'

The figure vanished, noiselessly, like a wraith.

'He's gone,' said Ginger. 'Come on, Biggles; let's get out of this. We're asking for it.'

'I'm inclined to agree with you,' conceded Biggles, and with his gun in his hand began backing slowly towards the water.

Ginger, expecting a shower of arrows any moment, followed him until he stopped behind a pile of buckled plates that had once been the bows of the *Cygnet*.

Biggles shrugged. 'Well, where do we go from here?'

'Home,' answered Ginger without hesitation. 'Quite obviously there's nothing we can do, and we should be stark raving mad to stay.'

'We'll go back to the others and talk it over,' decided Biggles.

Five minutes later they were in the cabin discussing the situation. Not, as Algy observed, that there was much to discuss, for on the face of it to start digging operations in such circumstances would, apart from being a waste of time, be sheer lunacy. 'The only people who know where the gold is, assuming they're still alive, are the crooks who buried it,' he concluded. 'We have at least located the wreck and the Air Commodore should well be satisfied with that. Let the people who want the gold make their own arrangements for fetching it. That's what I say.'

'Absolutely, old boy,' agreed Bertie. 'I'm with you, every time. I mean to say, we're not a bally bunch of navvies. Filthy business. The beastly place stinks.'

'There's no hurry, anyway,' stated Biggles. 'We'll brew a dish of tea and nibble a biscuit while we wait.'

'Wait! For what?' inquired Ginger.

'There's just a chance that if the fellow we saw watching us goes back and spreads the news, the Village Constable might come along to see what we're doing. I gather from what Thompson said he speaks a little English, in which case we could ask a few questions.'

Biggles' hope was more than fulfilled when, soon afterwards, not a native but a white man appeared on the beach. His style of dress revealed his calling and Biggles got up quickly.

'This is better still,' he said briskly. 'It must be Father Antoinne.'

Leaving Algy in charge of the aircraft the others made their way to where the priest, an incongruous figure against the savage background, stood watching. Gaunt and hollow-cheeked, his skin was that curious yellow-bronze tint that is the result of long years in malarial tropics, and Ginger looked at him with the respect to which such a man is entitled.

'Father Antoinne?' queried Biggles, as they drew near.

Looking a little surprised that his name should be known to a stranger, the priest bowed acknowledgment.

Biggles introduced himself and his companions.

'One of my boys told me you were here so I walked down to see if I could be of any assistance,' explained Father Antoinne. 'Are you in trouble?'

'No,' replied Biggles. 'We landed here deliberately. As a matter of fact we're interested in the wreck of this ship, having been sent out by the British Government to find it. Can you tell us anything about it?'

'Unfortunately, yes,' answered the priest. 'I say unfortunately,' he went on, 'because certain members of the crew have been responsible for a great deal of trouble here. What their purpose was I don't know. They did not behave like ordinary shipwrecked sailors. As a result of their behaviour I suspect most of them have lost their lives.'

'What happened?' prompted Biggles.

'I'm not entirely clear about the beginning because when the ship went ashore I was away in one of the outlying villages of my district,' continued Father Antoinne. 'And, I am sorry to say, the accounts of the natives are not to be trusted. As I understand it the ship went ashore in a storm, and the crew, mostly coloured men, for reasons best known to themselves, decided to attempt the formidable task of trying to reach Port Moresby, on the other side of the island. They passed through Kobe country unmolested. Indeed, some were given food. What happened to them afterwards I don't know, but as, against advice, they went on into the territory of the Gilkiks, I imagine they did not get far. The Gilkiks are a bad tribe. I don't know a single man who has survived a passage through their country.'

'What caused the trouble here?' questioned Biggles.

'Two white men, the captain of the ship and another. They remained here, in the Kobe village, which is not far away. They seemed disinclined to leave. Why, I must again plead ignorance.'

'You don't happen to know their names?'

'I may know the name of one. But let me tell you. According to my boys – for, you must understand, I was not here – these two men spent most of their time drinking and arguing. Considering how they were situated such folly is hardly to be believed. One day an argument ended in a terrible fist fight. As the victor walked away, the other, lying on the ground, took out a pistol and shot him dead. Upon this, the natives who saw it, being both excited and frightened, tried to seize him, but after shooting some of them he fled, snatching up his rifle as he went. It was shortly after this that I returned.'

'Why were the natives frightened?' inquired Biggles curiously.

'Because a white man had been killed. That is a serious matter, and they were afraid they would be blamed for the murder, which in due course would reach the ears of the authorities. They left the body where it lay. It was still there when I came back. I made them bury it. But before that I went through the dead man's pockets and found letters addressed to Blake.'

'Ah!' breathed Biggles. 'So it was Blake. Thank you, Father; that was what I wanted to know. It confirms that this wreck is the one I was looking for. Now I will tell you something which will explain much. Blake, with an accomplice named Diaz – the man who murdered him, no doubt – stole this ship. There was gold on board. They buried it, and presumably it's still here. That, we may suppose, was what the arguments were about. It also explains their reluctance to leave the place.'

'Gold,' said the priest softly, shaking his head. 'I might have guessed it; for where there is gold, too often there is trouble. This explains something else, for my tale is not yet finished. When the murderer of Blake fled he went into the Gilkik country, and, naturally, we supposed him to be dead. But it was not so. By what miracle he not only survived, but was able to enlist the aid of these incorrigible barbarians, is something beyond my understanding; but thus it was, for not long afterwards the Gilkiks attacked the Kobe village, and with them, shooting with his rifle, was this white villain.'

'Diaz, trying to get to the gold,' conjectured Biggles.

'I see now that could have been the reason, although there has never been any love between the two tribes,' said Father Antoinne.

'What happened?'

'The attack was beaten off, for the Kobes are stout fighters and were on their own ground. Other attacks followed, with the same result.'

'And Diaz is still with the Gilkiks?'

'As far as I know. Why does he stay with these dreadful people?'

'I think the answer to that is pretty clear,' replied Biggles. 'He knows where the gold is hidden and he's determined to have it. He must have realized that by now the police are looking for him. With money he could hide, get to America, or keep on the run. Without money he would be helpless. Aside from which he would be loath to abandon so much wealth, knowing that if once he left New Guinea he would find it difficult to get back.'

'Which means that we may expect more attacks,' rejoined the priest wearily. 'The Kobes seem to know that, for they are in their war-paint and the drums talk constantly. In that mood they are beyond my control. Indeed, they cannot control themselves. This renegade white man has undone the work of years.'

Biggles took a cigarette from his case, lit it, and considered the matter.

'What are you contemplating, my son?' asked the priest shrewdly, and with some anxiety.

'I am a police officer,' stated Biggles. 'I was wondering how I could get my hands on this murderer who is giving you and your people so much trouble. It's time he was brought to book.'

Father Antoinne looked doubtful. He did not reply.

Biggles looked up as if he had reached a decision. 'How far away is the Kobe village, Father?'

'About half a mile.'

'There is, I imagine, a chief, a headman, of the tribe.'

'Of course.'

'He won't resent my intrusion if I go to see him?'

'Not if you're with me.'

Biggles turned to Ginger and Bertie. 'Go to the aircraft. Tell Algy what's afoot. We're going to the village. Say he's to stand by with a gun trained on the beach ready for action. Bring back two automatic rifles, with ammunition, and the twelve-bore pump gun with buckshot cartridges.'

As Ginger and Bertie went off Biggles turned to the priest with an apologetic smile. 'I'm sorry, Father, if these arrangements are opposed to your principles, but I have a job to do, and my preparations are dictated by the circumstances. These weapons will not of course be used except under pressure from a hostile force that threatens our lives.'

'I understand,' said the priest. He was standing in a listening attitude.

'What can you hear?' asked Biggles.

'The drums are talking. Listen.'

Biggles waited. Then he said: 'Do you know what they're saying?'

'Yes. They say white men have landed on the beach by the wreck.'

'Is that message intended just for the Kobes?'

Father Antoinne shrugged. 'It would be understood by any native who hears it.'

'The Gilkiks?'

'Certainly.'

Biggles looked alarmed. 'You realize what the effect of that will be?'

'In what way?'

'If Diaz is told he will guess what white men are doing here –'

'And – ?'

'He'll make a last desperate attempt to get the only thing that matters to him – the gold.'

The priest's eyes opened wide. 'I didn't think of that.' he admitted.

'Am I correct in supposing that the Gilkiks couldn't get to this beach without passing through Kobe country?'

'Definitely. In this jungle even the natives can move only by following the tracks. The one that leads to this creek passes through the Kobe village. I see now that is why the village was attacked. This man Diaz was really trying to get here.'

'That's how I understood it,' returned Biggles. He turned to where Ginger and Bertie were coming ashore with the weapons. 'Come on,' he said tersely. 'Things are likely to happen. We're going to the village and we've no time to lose. Lead the way, Father,' he concluded, taking the shot-gun from Ginger, loading it, and putting some loose cartridges in his pocket.

*

The way lay through the mangroves, as they realized it must, for the beach on which they stood, on the landward side, was entirely hemmed in by the grotesque trees. They also knew what sort of ordeal lay before them, and here again their fears were justified, However, there was no alternative.

For much of the way they struggled knee-deep through noisome mud, their weight causing foul-looking bubbles to rise and, bursting, release gases that stank abominably. And this was not the worst. Where broad pools of stagnant water occurred they had to proceed by stepping from one hooped root to another. These were damp and slippery. Sometimes one would break, dropping the traveller waist deep in slime. There is perhaps no form of pedestrian travel more strenuous or more revolting than through a mangrove swamp. The heat was suffocating.

Fortunately these conditions prevailed only for about twenty minutes, when the party, streaked with mud and dripping with sweat, reached the rising ground where the swamp gave way to ordinary jungle. Forward ran a narrow track, dim under the interlacing branches of lush palms and forest trees.

'Phew,' gasped Biggles, pausing to mop his streaming face. 'We're well out of that.'

Wiping condensation from his eyeglass Bertie gave his opinion softly and without passion. 'You know, old boy,' said he, 'there are times when I think I must be off my chump; completely off my rocker. Why, I ask myself, do I submit my body to these ghastly tortures. Soldiers, having more sense, would have demanded a Bailey bridge.'

'And a canteen on the far side,' put in Ginger, grinning through the grime on his face.

'Quit trying to fool me,' bantered Biggles. 'You love the going when it's tough. Let's keep mobile.'

Shouldering their weapons they went on, the priest leading.

The drums could now be heard plainly, their volume deepening and their tempo rising.

'In a minute there will be fighting.' Father Antoinne flung the words over his shoulder and set a faster pace.

Ginger marvelled that a man of his age and impaired constitution could move at such a rate. It was as much as he could do to keep up.

In spite of their efforts the assault on the village had been launched before they could reach it, an uproar of yells, howls and a noise like the barking of dogs announcing the onset. Through the din came the vicious twang of bowstrings and an occasional rifle shot.

'Sounds as if Diaz is there,' said Biggles, and dashed forward to where a patch of sunlight showed the end of the track. He reached it, with the others close behind, just as a pack of shrieking savages came rushing towards the same spot from the opposite direction. It was a nasty moment, for whether the men were Kobes or Gilkiks, Biggles and his friends had of course no means of knowing. The blacks, seeing them, stopped dead, huddling, crouching, staring. Their great mops of hair, their faces and bodies daubed with white clay, their mouths stained scarlet with betel-nut, and with boars' tusks thrust through their nostrils, they presented a picture of bestial savagery not easily forgotten. Some of the men carried spears, others heavy six-foot bows.

Father Antoinne saved what might have been an ugly situation by running forward, hands raised, crying out something in what was presumably the native language.

'Don't shoot, they're my people,' he told Biggles quickly.

The warriors, recognizing him, again broke into a furious barking, and turning about, rushed back into the village from which a cloud of smoke was rising. The white men followed, and there on the open ground before them saw a battle raging.

To Ginger, who took in the scene in one comprehensive

stare, it was clear that the Kobes, recognizable by their white war-paint, were getting the worst of it. Several of their houses were on fire, and the warriors, in little groups, were fighting with their backs to the walls, or the flames, as the case might be. One reason for this, or so it seemed to Ginger, was the fact that they were out-numbered. He was in fact, shocked by the number of their enemies, easily distinguishable by having red-smeared bodies; and his first thought was that they themselves would be lucky to get out of the affair alive. He, at all events, had not expected anything on quite such a scale; and he suspected that Biggles must have thought on the same lines, or he would hardly have gone into the business without any sort of plan.

However, spears and bows and arrows are one thing, and modern automatic weapons are another. 'Steady with those rifles,' shouted Biggles. 'If you must shoot, shoot low.' With that he raised his gun and opened fire.

Now a rifle is a deadly weapon, but it can fire only a single bullet at a time, and at a single target. A twelve-bore shot gun, firing a small handful of pellets, at a range of sixty or seventy yards has a wide spread; and although the shots may not be lethal they can sting pretty hard. And this the Gilkiks soon discovered. Half a dozen shots were sufficient to alter the entire situation. The attackers leapt high into the air as the leaden hail smacked into their bare skins. Some fell. Some danced screaming, dropping their weapons as they clutched at the spots where they had been hit. They may have thought these trivial wounds were fatal. At any rate they were soon hopping and jumping back towards the forest from which they had emerged. Biggles gave them a few parting shots, the pellets rattling on the heavy-leafed foliage.

At this juncture there was reason to suppose that the conflict was as good as over; but this was not so. The Kobes, who must have been astonished, and not a little gratified, by the turn of events, now took the initiative, and set about their retreating foes clearly determined to have their revenge. This put an end to any further shooting, for in the general mix-up it was impossible to pick a target.

Ginger, who had been keeping an eye open for Diaz – for the crack of a rifle had indicated his presence – now saw him for the first time. With a number of Gilkiks he had apparently been operating among the houses. Seeing himself in danger of being abandoned he now appeared, running towards the forest, with some Kobes in pursuit. For a moment it looked as if he would succeed in reaching cover, for although Ginger let out a warning shout and half raised his rifle, he hesitated to shoot. As it happened there was no need. Diaz was within five yards of the trees when an arrow, fired by one of the pursuing Kobes, buried itself between his shoulders and brought him down with a crash.

With a cry of horror Father Antoinne hurried towards him. The others followed slowly, alert for danger, for although by this time the village was practically deserted, a lot of yelling just inside the forest suggested that the Gilkiks might make a counter-attack. Moreover, stray arrows were still flying.

'Watch how you go,' cautioned Biggles.

With rifles at the ready they approached the spot where Father Antoinne was on his knees beside the stricken pirate. Hearing them coming he half turned and made made a sign that could only mean one thing. Biggles stopped, and halted the others. 'There's nothing much you can do for a man with one of those ghastly double-barbed arrows in his vitals,' he said quietly. 'Whether you leave it in or try to get it out it comes to the same thing.'

Silent and subdued they watched the priest administer the last rites, and presently cover the face of the man whose misdeeds had brought him only a miserable death.

Father Antoinne joined them. 'It's all over,' said he, sombrely. 'Knowing he was dying the unhappy man confessed everything. The gold is still where it was buried. Standing alone at the end of the mangroves are three sago palms. You will find everything just under the ground at the foot of the largest.'

'Thank you,' acknowledged Biggles. 'For the time being it can remain there. I'll return home and report the matter to the owners, who will no doubt send a vessel to fetch it. Is there anything we can do for you?'

'There's nothing you can do here. In such cases as this I know from experience that it is better to leave the natives to settle their own affairs. For a time they will be even beyond my control.' The priest thought for a moment. 'If you have any foodstuffs, or medical stores that will not now be required, I would be glad to have them. I am always short of such things.'

'We have quite a lot of stuff on board that we shan't need – thanks largely to you,' Biggles answered. 'We'll put it all on the beach, if you can send some of your boats to fetch it.'

'Certainly, and thank you very much.'

'Thank you, sir,' returned Biggles. 'And now, as you

say there's nothing we can do here, if you'll excuse us we'll get back to the beach. My friend in the aircraft must have heard the shooting and will be in a state of anxiety.'

'Naturally.'

They shook hands, and leaving the priest, a lonely figure with one hand raised in a valedictory blessing, standing on the track, they turned their faces towards the sea.

3

THE ADVENTURE OF THE LUMINOUS CLAY

'BIGGLESWORTH, I want you to meet Sir James Randal and Professor Lovejoy,' said Air Commodore Raymond, as his chief operational pilot entered the Special Air Section Office at Scotland Yard.

Biggles acknowledged the introductions. Sir James was an austere, distinguished-looking man, but it was with difficulty that he restrained a smile when shaking hands with the Professor, whose untidy dress and horn-rimmed spectacles recalled inevitably the proverbial absent-minded professor of funny stories.

'As you are probably aware,' went on the Air Commodore, 'Sir James is one of our leading atomic research specialists. He is now engaged in the adaptation of that power for commercial uses. Professor Lovejoy is, of course, the celebrated naturalist and explorer. They have come here, at the suggestion of another department, with a request for our co-operation in an enterprise that is unusual, to say the least of it. I will ask Sir James to tell you about it, after which you will please give us your views as to the practicability of the undertaking.'

Biggles turned to the scientist.

'We in this country are engaged in a race, a race to be first in world markets with a practical atomic power unit,' explained Sir James. 'You will appreciate that the country first in the field with such a device would at once be able to put itself in a happy position economically. Its export value could hardly be over-estimated.'

'I understand that, sir,' said Biggles, wondering – in view of previous experience – what secret had been stolen or mislaid.

'Very well,' resumed the scientist. 'I must now tell you that there is a certain highly complex substance vitally essential to the progress of our experiments. Let us call it Blue Clay. The manufacture of it, even a few grammes, is a long and costly process. It is, in fact, akin to radium. We are always being held up pending the delivery of fresh supplies. I doubt if it ever occurred to anyone that the stuff might exist in a natural form, but thanks to Professor Lovejoy that surprising fact has now been established beyond any doubt. There is, he asserts, an almost unlimited quantity waiting to be collected. The importance of this discovery, which of course we have not made public, could not be exaggerated.'

'Where is this remarkable deposit?' queried Biggles, who by this time had a good idea of what was coming.

'Before I answer that question I really must disclaim *all* the credit for the discovery,' declared the Professor. 'The truth is, I didn't know what I had found, which is not to be wondered at considering the extraordinary circumstances in which the thing came about. With a naturalist friend, who is in the happy position of being able to afford a deep sea yacht, I was cruising in the Pacific. Studying the eggs of some gulls that nested on an islet which happened to come under our observation, we made the startling discovery that they had the property of being luminous – or to be quite accurate, that the *shells* were luminous. On my return home I made a point of this in a paper I read to the Royal Society. Sir James was present. This resulted in some of my specimens being analyzed. This revealed that they contained a small amount of Blue Clay. Blue Clay itself is luminous. The eggs have a tinge of blue in them. I noticed some bluish-looking earth when I was on the islet, but as I was only there in daylight I did not perceive the luminosity. Putting two and two together, so to speak, we have come to this conclusion. The gulls that nest on this particular islet must swallow minute quantities of blue clay in the grit which they eat either for purposes of digestion or to form the shells of their eggs. As a result, these birds have the unique faculty of laying luminous eggs. Isn't that an astonishing story?'

'It certainly is,' agreed Biggles.

Sir James stepped in. 'It seems absurd to go on wasting precious time and money manufacturing something which can be picked up on the ground in almost any quantity. One container of Blue Clay would be sufficient to put us years ahead of any possible competitor.'

'I imagine this islet is in a remote spot,' said Biggles.

'It is in mid-Pacific. One of a small archipelago that lies some seven or eight hundred miles from the west coast of Central South America. Geographically, it might be regarded as a distant offshoot of the Galapagos group.'

'Is the archipelago – the Blue Clay group – inhabited?'

'One island only. It is the main island, but even so it is small, and not very productive, for which reason, no doubt, no one has ever bothered about it. Consequently the natives, thought to be of Polynesian extraction, are backward – to put it nicely – and have a reputation for discouraging visitors. The Blue Earth islet, which I have named Gull Rock, is some miles away. It is a mere volcanic pimple, like a hollow tooth sticking up out of the sea. All the islands are volcanic, as indeed are the Galapagos, which within living memory have been subject to volcanic disturbances – earthquakes and eruptions. Gull Rock, by the way, is not shown on the chart, so it may well be of recent formation. It could even be one of these islands that come and go. There are several in the Pacific. A ship sights one, puts it on the chart, but when the next ship passes it isn't there. There is no proper anchorage at Gull Islet. It rises sheer from deep water.'

'But it's possible to land on it without any great difficulty?'

'Providing there isn't a heavy sea running. In that case it would be dangerous, if not impossible. Frankly, I'm afraid it may disappear at any moment. Hence the urgency of another visit.'

'Assuming it's still there, all we have to do is land and collect a bucket of Blue Clay. Is that it?'

Scientist and explorer glanced at each other, then looked at the Air Commodore, who, turning to Biggles, remarked dryly. 'Well, it isn't quite as simple as that.'

'What's the snag?'

'The snag is the question of ownership. The group happens to be one of those to which, in these days of radio and aircraft refuelling stations, several countries now lay claim. If it were known that one of the islands had a particular value, and we had made a raid on it, there might be an international rumpus, and we don't want that.'

'I would have said that the people who have most right to the islands are those who live there,' asserted Biggles.

'And many people would agree with you,' averred Sir James. 'But such claims are brushed aside when international politics are involved.'

The Air Commodore interposed. 'The point is, we don't want to start anything. As far as the natives are concerned Gull Rock is just another dot in the ocean. They know nothing of the value of Blue Clay and wouldn't be able to handle it if they did. No doubt they'd be happy to sell the lot for a few fish-hooks. Wherefore, if we could collect some of the Clay without anybody knowing anything about it, there should be no heartburning. The thing is, and can remain, a top secret.'

'And the idea is for me to go out and do the collecting?'

'Yes. Providing the secret hasn't leaked out, and we have no reason to suppose that it has, there should be no great difficulty about it.'

Biggles nodded. 'The thing looks simple, but it's almost uncanny the way simple things can produce unforeseen difficulties. However, we'll deal with them should any arise.'

'I'll leave it to you to make your own arrangements. Be as quick as you can.'

'Do you mind if I come with you?' asked Professor Lovejoy.

Biggles hesitated.

'I might be useful in several ways. I would recognize the Blue Clay for instance, and should we have occasion to land on the main island, having some knowledge of

Polynesian, I could talk to the people. Without me you might have difficulties in finding the right islet.'

'All right, sir,' consented Biggles. 'You come at your own risk, of course.'

'That's understood.'

The arrangements for Operation Gull Rock presented no difficulty to Biggles and his pilots, to whom long-distance flights had, from experience, become a matter of routine. Lists of everything likely to be needed were ready to hand. Everyone had his own particular job and did it, from the laying on of stores and spares to the investigation of probable weather conditions and the plotting of courses. Consequently, within a fortnight, the flying-boat selected for the assignment, the old Sunderland that had served them so well, was within striking distance of its objective. The story given out at refuelling points was that the Sunderland was a survey ship, trying out new routes.

Ginger, sitting next to Biggles in the control cabin, staring at the pitiless distances ahead, gave a sigh of relief when the lonely group of islands came into view almost directly on their course, for long periods of over-water flying are apt to become monotonous and there is always a risk of missing a small mark in a great expanse of ocean.

Biggles flew on, surveying the several islets and islands as they crept up over the edge of the world. The Professor had provided him with a rough sketch of Gull Island, so he anticipated no difficulty in identifying it when it came into view. He failed to find it, although its relative position in the group had been plotted. At last losing some height, he said: 'There's something wrong here. Better ask the Professor to come forward and –'

At that moment Algy appeared. 'That's it, over there,' he said, pointing.

'But that isn't like the sketch he gave me,' protested Biggles.

'No. He says it's altered, but he's quite sure that's it.'

'Okay. We'll soon settle it.'

As Biggles began to glide down, Ginger, in a puzzled voice remarked: 'There's something going on down there. Look at the way the gulls are behaving. Well, blow me down! I can see people – natives; there are their canoes, lined up against the shelf. They must have come over from the main island.'

'Good thing we've got the Professor with us.'

'Are you going down?'

'Of course. The sea looks flat calm, that's one good thing. I thought we'd be lucky to get through without something unexpected turning up. We'll lie off until we hear what the Professor thinks about it.'

Biggles brought the Sunderland round, and making a smooth landing about half a mile off shore, taxied on until he was only half the distance from the Rock with everything in plain view. There must have been five or six war canoes drawn up against the shelf of rock that was the most convenient landing place. Ashore, nearly a hundred natives were staring at the flying-boat. Disturbed gulls were wheeling round the rock with a clamour of protest.

By this time the Professor was talking to Biggles, a hint of apology in his voice. 'Please don't think I deliberately deceived you about the natives,' he said. 'I'm afraid we've arrived at an unfortunate moment. I can't think this is an ordinary native outing. It looks more as if some sort of ceremony was going on.'

'You're sure it's the right rock? It isn't much like the one you sketched for me.'

'It's the right one, but it has changed since I was last here,' declared the Professor. 'It was higher than this. Moreover, it appears to have split. There must have been a volcanic disturbance.'

'What's the best thing to do?'

'Will the aircraft ride comfortably where she is?'

'With conditions as they are, yes. But if a sea gets up, without any sort of anchorage we should have to get airborne.'

'Then I suggest we stay where we are for the time being, in the hope that the natives will return to their home island very soon. It would be dangerous to land.'

'What makes you think that?'

'If those people were in a friendly mood they would have paddled out to welcome us before this. The way they just stand and stare is always a bad sign.'

'All right,' assented Biggles. 'We'll post a guard, and take the opportunity to have something to eat.'

The day wore on without any change in the situation. The sea remained calm but the natives gave no sign of departure. The Professor, who had remarked on the absence of fish round the flying-boat, pointed to some dead ones floating by. There was also a quantity of grey scum. These, he said, were sure signs of a volcanic disturbance not far away. That, no doubt, was what caused the rock to sink.

'As long as it doesn't blow up –' began Ginger.

'I don't think there's much fear of that,' interposed the Professor. 'It's more likely that the rock will continue to sink quietly into the water.'

Towards evening a canoe, with a dozen men in it

came paddling cautiously towards the aircraft. This suited Biggles, who was getting impatient and anxious to know how long the brown men intended to stay. But not being prepared to take chances of a surprise attack he started the engines, and leaving them ticking over, posted Bertie in the centre turret with a rifle. The Professor stood by in order to parley.

Apparently the natives were not taking any chances either, for as soon as they were within hailing distance they rested on their paddles. Their manner was neither friendly nor hostile. In this situation the Professor engaged them in what appeared to be a difficult conversation, at the end of which the canoe was paddled back to the rock.

'What was that all about?' asked Biggles.

'They want us to go away. They say we've brought disaster on them by annoying their gods. The fire god has almost destroyed their island, so they've come here to placate him with sacrifices.'

'In other words there's been an eruption.'

'That's about the English of it.'

'And we've got to fiddle about here until they decide to go.'

'I'm afraid so. It would be folly to attempt a landing.'

'Well, I suppose we shall just have to wait,' said Biggles in a resigned voice. 'I don't mind admitting I'd rather be somewhere else. An undersea disturbance would mean a tidal wave, and that wouldn't be funny.'

When the sun sank into the sea and darkness settled swiftly over the strange scene, a possible reason for the natives' behaviour became manifest, particularly in view of the association of the fire god. On the rock appeared a startling phenomenon. Up and down the spire-like shape glowed a tongue of unearthly fire, like a vivid neon sign, to shed an uncanny light on the mirror of water below.

When the Professor exclaimed that it was the Blue Clay no one disputed it. It was hard to imagine what else it could be. 'What has happened is,' he stated, 'the rock has been split by an internal convulsion exposing the inner core, which appears to be composed entirely of the Blue Clay. What a truly amazing spectacle.'

'If it has split the whole thing may topple over,' said Algy.

'I think that's quite likely,' agreed the Professor.

'The natives must be crazy to stay where they are. They can't realize their danger.'

'They're probably scared out of their wits. I can only think that something awful must have happened on their own island or they'd go back to it.'

'Maybe they will, when they've finished their sacrificing,' suggested Bertie hopefully.

'That scum we saw floating was certainly lava thrown up by a volcano,' said the Professor.

'If the position tomorrow remains unchanged we'll fly round and see if we can locate it,' returned Biggles. 'Meanwhile, we might as well turn in and get some sleep.'

In the event, this suggestion was never followed up, for some time later, while they were still sitting in the cabin discussing the matter, they were startled by a long low rumble, like distant thunder. It was impossible to say from what direction it came, but from the fact that the aircraft rocked a little, it was thought to be nearer than it had sounded.

'I don't like this,' muttered Algy positively.

'Nobody likes it,' answered Biggles. 'But having come so far it goes against the grain to run away without even knowing what we're running from. The Rock is still there, anyhow. I'm going to take a canful of that clay when I go.'

Ginger could not recall a more uncomfortable night than the one that followed. Alarming might be a better word. The rumbles were repeated at intervals, and each time the aircraft moved uneasily. Once it seemed to shudder.

'I swear that was right underneath us,' asserted Bertie. 'I've heard people talk about sitting on a volcano. This must be it.' As if to confirm his words a clatter of falling rock took them all to a window. But the Rock was still there, a wonderful but terrifying spectacle. A smell of sulphur was noticeable.

'If those wretched natives are still there they must be scared stiff,' opined Algy.

'So am I, old boy, if it comes to that,' responded Bertie warmly. 'They must be nuts to stay.'

'That goes for us, too,' put in Ginger. 'I can see no sign of the silly fellows,' murmured the Professor.

The first grey of dawn did nothing to allay their fears. More patches of thick grey scum appeared on the water, which here and there began to writhe in little whirlpools. The Rock was still there, but it was noticeably lower in the water. As the sky brightened it could be seen that the natives had gone.

'That's all we were waiting for,' said Biggles briskly. 'Let's get cracking, and move ourselves from the top of a kettle that sounds as if it's about to boil over. Launch the dinghy. Get the can, Ginger.'

The Professor let out a yell. 'It's going!'

They all spun round to see the Rock sinking slowly into the sea. Ripples rolled away from it.

'Beaten at the post, by Jove!' muttered Bertie.

Biggles went through to the control cabin and started the engines.

'It's stopped,' shouted Algy.

'Then let us hope it'll stay put for just a few minutes longer,' said Biggles grimly, edging the machine nearer.

The atmosphere became tense, for it was obvious to everyone that nature was about to have another convulsion, and that it might happen at any moment. Biggles did not attempt to deceive them, or himself as was plain, from the expression on his face.

He took the Sunderland to within a hundred yards of the dying rock and then moved swiftly. He snatched up the metal container brought to hold the Blue Clay, got into the dinghy and pushed it clear. 'If she starts to boil over before I get back, get clear. Don't wait for me,' he ordered crisply.

'But –'

'Do as you're told.'

'Okay,' obeyed Ginger, who had started to get into the dinghy. He knew that Biggles in his present mood would brook no argument.

They all watched him paddle to the Rock. He seemed to be a long time getting there, and even longer time making a precarious landing on the now almost vertical face of rock. Actually, by the clock on the instrument panel, he was away less than half an hour; but even that can seem an eternity when there is a likelihood of any second being the last.

The trouble was, the Rock was not true rock, but soft tufa of volcanic origin that crumbled away in Biggles' hand when he tried to climb to the split just above his head in order to get at the clay. Once he started a minor avalanche and looked like going with it into the sea, from which wreaths of steam were beginning to coil. The flimsy tufa floated like pumice-stone, which it would become when it hardened. To Algy's concern it floated out to the Sunderland, for he wondered what effect it would have on the keel if he had to take off in a hurry.

However, Biggles finally achieved his object, and with the canister under his arm slid back to the dinghy.

Beads of perspiration broke out on Ginger's forehead as he watched, for it was obviously going to be touch and go. The rumblings were ominous. More and more thick grey scum came floating up from the sea bed to swirl, smoking, on the surface. More than once, on his way back, Biggles had to clear a passage through it with his paddle. Sulphur reeked, and the others could see him coughing.

Even before he reached the aircraft the Rock had resumed its slow slide to oblivion. The vortex slowed the dinghy, and at one time looked like dragging it back. Then Bertie threw a line; Biggles caught it, and the sluggish little craft was dragged in. Biggles scrambled aboard. 'Abandon the dinghy,' he panted. 'Get off,' he told Algy.

But the scum was now so thick that there could be no question of taking off through it. All Algy could do was force a passage in the manner of an ice-breaker. But the stuff cleared as they got farther from the danger zone, and to the the great relief of everyone the Sunderland bellowed its way into the atmosphere.

Looking back, Ginger could no longer see Gull Rock.

'By gosh! You were only just in time,' he told Biggles. 'She's gone.'

'Best thing that could happen,' declared Biggles mopping his streaming face. 'No one else will be tempted to come to this stinking place. You might fetch me a bowl of water. I'd feel better for a wash.'

The Sunderland droned on, its bows towards the mainland.

4

THE FLYING
CRUSADERS

OUTSIDE the Air Police Operations Headquarters a summer sun glinted on the polished surfaces of sundry aircraft parked on the concrete apron. Through them, cap
in hand, walked Air Constable Algy Lacey after a routine test flight. 'Seems a pity to spend a day like this
fiddling with filing cabinets,' he observed, striding into
the office where Air Constables 'Ginger' Hebblethwaite
and 'Bertie' Lissie were working on index cards.

'You can all go down to the country for the week-end
if you like,' offered Biggles from his desk, where he was
dealing with the morning mail. 'I may take a run out
myself.'

'And do what?' inquired Ginger.

Biggles smiled. 'We could have a busman's holiday
by looking at some of the bamboo and piano-wire con-
traptions in which people staggered into the atmosphere
before instruments were invented.'

'Where's this?' inquired Ginger. 'I've always wanted
to fly a bird-cage.'

'Mancroft Castle. Sir Giles Mancroft was one of the
very early pioneers. When he got too old for the game

he spent his money – too much, it seems, since he's having to sell up – making a collection of the early types of aircraft. He kept them in flying trim, too. I have an invitation to the auction on Saturday. Seems a pity to have to break up what must be a unique aviation museum. Incidentally, I see the sale includes the Flying Crusader, the machine in which, with a bit of luck, Sir Giles might have been first across the Channel. I seem to remember there was some trouble about that machine a few years ago, but I forget the details. I must look them up. I have a note here, too, from a fellow named Smithers who used to be one of my mechanics in the war. He says he now works with Sir Giles and wants to see me. Presumably his visit has something to do with the sale. I hope he doesn't expect me to buy these old crates.'

Biggles' fears were not realized, for some time later, when Smithers arrived, it was soon clear that his journey had been prompted by motives altogether different. 'Seeing that you're coming to the auction, sir, and hearing you were in the Air Police, I took a chance that you might be able to help me,' he explained.

'How did you know I was going to the auction?'

'I posted the invitations and saw your name on one,' admitted Smithers frankly.

'And in what way can I help you?'

'By clearing my father's name. With the old Crusader being sold it'll be the last chance.'

'Suppose you sit down and tell us about it,' suggested Biggles.

'Well, sir, you must understand that there are two Flying Crusaders – or there were,' began the ex-airman. 'One is a 'plane and the other is a picture. No doubt one was called after the other. But I'd better warn you right away that the business that I'm going to tell you about, in which they were both involved, takes a bit of believing now. You'll wonder, as I do sometimes, why this and that wasn't done at the time; but the war started bang in the middle of the affair and the police had something else to do; for which reason, I suppose, the case was soon dropped and hardly mentioned in the papers. The first Flying Crusader was a picture presented to one of Sir Giles' ancestors by the Tsar of Russia at the time of the Crusades. It shows a knight in armour on a winged horse. It was quite small, but as it was painted by the most famous artist of the time I reckon it would be worth something today; enough to save Sir Giles having to sell the estate, if he could get it back.'

'Where is the picture now?' inquired Biggles.

'That's what we'd like to know,' answered Smithers sadly. 'It disappeared in circumstances that really cost my father his life.'

'How did that come about?'

'It was like this, sir. It happened at a house-party just two days before the war. Sir Giles gave the party to people interested in aviation to show off the old machines. One of the guests was an American named Silberman, who claimed to have been in the famous Escadrille Lafayette, the American squadron that fought for France in the early days of the first war. According to him at the inquiry this is what happened.'

'Your father was employed by Sir Giles I take it?'

'Yes, sir, first as a mechanic and afterwards as his butler.'

'I see. Go on.'

'Silberman said that after he had gone to bed he

found he had left his cigarette case in the library and went down to get it. The first thing he saw was that the Flying Crusader picture had been cut out of its frame. The window over-looking the park was open. From it he saw a light moving near the canvas hangars in which the old aircraft were housed. Thinking it might be the thief he ran down and caught the man, who turned out to be my father. According to Silberman my father attacked him. There was a fight, and that part was true, because not only did it end in my father being so terribly knocked about that he never recovered, but Silberman himself was in hospital for some time. A gamekeeper heard the noise and rushed in to find my father on the ground, and Silberman leaning against the old Crusader; which is why I think the 'plane had something to do with it. They were both carried off to hospital.'

'Do I understand your father died without saying what happened?'

'Yes, sir. He had a head injury and never fully re-covered consciousness up to the time he died a week or two later. All he could do was mutter something about the Flying Crusader. Of course, he wouldn't think of taking the picture. What made things look bad for him was, he was one of the few people who knew about the treasure supposed to be linked up with the painting. There was an old legend in the family that the picture was actually the key to a treasure which the first Sir Giles was supposed to have brought back from Russia. My father often suggested to the present Sir Giles that they took the picture out of the frame to have a closer look; but he wouldn't do anything about it. He'd just laugh and say the story was a lot of romantic nonsense.'

'I see,' said Biggles slowly. 'What was your father

supposed to be doing in the hangar when Silberman caught him there?'

'It was suggested that he was about to make off with the picture. To me that didn't make sense, but the way it was put at the inquiry it didn't sound so unreasonable because there were cars in the hangar. There wasn't room for all the guests' cars in the garage, so some were put in the hangars.'

'And what about the picture?'

'It was never found. There was a search made for it, but it was only half-hearted. The war was on and the police had something else to do. Sir Giles himself went off to war. Being on the reserve I had to go. Silberman went back to America and the whole thing sort of fizzled out. Nobody really bothered. By the time my father died people were thinking more about being bombed.'

'And what's your view of it?'

'I say it was Silberman who took the picture, not my father,' declared Smithers. 'It was the other way round. My father caught *him*. That's why I've come to you now, sir. Silberman killed my father to get that picture, and it struck me that if he hears about the sale he'll turn up on Saturday. That's if, as I believe, the old 'plane has something to do with the mystery.'

'How do you know he hasn't already got the picture?'

'I don't see how he could have got it. If he had, we'd have heard about it by now. Something tells me that picture is linked up with the 'plane, and it's a long time since anyone saw the old Crusader. You see, by the time Silberman was out of hospital the war was in full swing. The castle was requisitioned by the government, so the old machines were dismantled and stored in the cellars with the furniture. Silberman couldn't have got to them there. The auction on Saturday will be the first time the 'planes have been seen in public.

'You're not suggesting that Silberman was going to *fly* away with the picture?'

'No. Why should he? His car was one of those parked in the hangar. I say Silberman was making for his car when my father caught up with him. He never got to the car. The picture wasn't in it, because the cars were searched the next day. Silberman, being in hospital, couldn't have got to it to move anything.'

Biggles considered the matter. 'All right, Smithers,' he said. 'I see what you're driving at. We'll come down on Saturday and have a look round. By the way, have any of the machines been in the air recently?'

Smithers smiled. 'Only the Flying Crusader. Yesterday, believe it or not, Sir Giles decided for old time's sake to have a last flip – only inside the grounds, of course. We put some fuel and oil in her. I didn't think she'd start; but lo and behold, off she went like a bird, and Sir Giles did a circuit at about ten feet.'

'Good show,' acknowledged Biggles, smiling. 'Now I shall certainly make a point of coming down on Saturday to have a look at her.'

When Smithers had gone Biggles turned to the others. 'If only for a day out I shall have to go down and put in a bid for this gallant old kite.'

'Do you really want it?' inquired Ginger.

Biggles shook his head. 'No. We've no room for antiques. But if somebody else wants her he'll have to bid against me; and the higher the bidding goes the more interested shall I become.'

'You mean, if the picture thief is there you'll force him to show his hand?' suggested Algy.

'Either that or I'm going to land myself with an expensive souvenir in the shape of an extremely obsolete aircraft. Actually, you'd better do the bidding, Ginger. Someone in the crowd may recognize me and ask awkward questions if I'm seen doing it. Keep an eye on me, and keep bidding till I signal you to stop. I shall want to see who's bidding against you if the price gets high. You others can keep your eyes skinned, too.

'D'you seriously expect Silberman to be there, old boy?' inquired Bertie shrewdly, polishing his eyeglass.

'I don't know about that,' replied Biggles pensively. 'He might be. If he comes he'll probably be in some sort of disguise. After what happened at Mancroft Castle he'd hardly have the brass face to be seen in public, bidding for a machine near which, after all, he did kill a man. That would look mighty suspicious to some people. Newspapers have long memories, and reporters would soon be asking questions which Silberman might find embarrassing. He won't overlook that, you may be sure. We'll go down in the car.'

*

Mancroft Castle turned out to be a magnificent country seat set in parkland not far from the flat expanse of the Fens; but to Biggles and his assistants the point of interest was not the scenery but the row of veteran 'planes parked on a simple airstrip that fronted two dilapidated canvas hangars. Gathered round them were interested spectators, a sprinkling of pioneer pilots and prospective buyers representing museums and aero clubs. Looking at the amazing structures of wood, canvas and wire, Ginger found it hard to believe that these, in their day, had been the queens of the air; that from them, in a lifetime, had been developed the high performance aircraft now annihilating space in every corner of the earth.

In a brief conversation with Sir Giles, to whom Biggles made himself known, they learned that while none of the machines was likely to qualify for a Certificate of Airworthiness, every one had flown, and could still, at any rate, get off the ground. He confirmed that he had flown the Flying Crusader the previous day. 'It would be a tragedy to see them go on the scrap heap,' he said sadly. 'I'm hoping most of them will end their days in museums.'

'I suppose you never heard anything more of the Flying Crusader picture that disappeared?' prompted Biggles. 'I've been refreshing my memory from the police files.'

'No,' answered Sir Giles. 'It's gone for good, I'm afraid. Like these machines, that unhappy business belongs to history. I named my machine after the picture, of course. I'm afraid poor old Smithers must have gone out of his mind and hidden the picture somewhere for safety. He seemed to have a curious regard for it. The other man in the case, Silberman, went back to the States and I lost touch with him.'

'He isn't in the States now,' returned Biggles. 'I happen to know that the Anti-American Activities Committee are looking for him.'

Apparently Sir Giles did not hear, or the significance of what Biggles had said was lost on him, for with a quick 'Excuse me, the sale is beginning,' he strode off.

In a somewhat depressing atmosphere Biggles and his friends watched aircraft that had made history being knocked down at prices lower than a junk dealer would have paid for old cars. The only brisk bidding was when a film director bought an early Farman to use as a prototype in a film he was making.

'The Crusader's next,' muttered Ginger looking at his catalogue.

'Keep your eyes open, everybody,' reminded Biggles.

Bidding for the Flying Crusader started well, but by the time the one hundred pounds mark had been reached Ginger was alone with a young man who called his offers in an American accent. The keenness of the duel after the previous desultory sales did not fail to attract attention, and as the price rose Biggles noticed an expression of growing embarrassment on the young American's face. Ginger, too, began to look worried when he reached two hundred pounds, and still Biggles had made no sign. Suddenly the American turned away and after a brief pause the auctioneer's hammer fell. The Flying Crusader had been knocked down to Ginger for £220, the highest figure of the day.

'What shall I tell the reporters if they question me?' Ginger asked Biggles.

'Say you represent the Air Ministry, which in a way is true enough,' answered Biggles. 'You can also let it be known that as the aircraft has petrol in her tank you intend to fly it to its new home tomorrow – you needn't say where.'

Ginger looked alarmed. 'Fly it? Are you kidding?'

'No. She'll fly. You heard what Sir Giles said?'

'What's the idea?'

'I want to encourage somebody, possibly our young American friend, to make a final effort to get hold of the Crusader before it disappears for good. Meanwhile it can go back into the hangar. I shan't take my eyes off it. We'll take turns to watch. I can see Smithers over there. I want to speak to him. Get the machine under cover and put the car handy behind the hangar in case we need it.'

*

Safeguarding the Flying Crusader turned out to be a long and tiresome vigil, for not until the first grey of dawn showed in the sky beyond the open front of the hangar was there any sign of an intruder. Then a figure, moving silently, showed for a moment silhouetted against the paling stars.

Just as quietly Biggles moved. His torch cut a wedge of light in the gloom revealing the startled face of the young American. Indeed, such was his confusion that it was apparent he was not accustomed to questionable nocturnal practices.

'Are you looking for something?' asked Biggles quietly.

'I – well – I was – er – just having a last look at the old crate,' stammered the new arrival.

Biggles' voice hardened. 'Funny time to choose. You'll have to give a more convincing explanation than that in court. I'm a police officer.'

'Police!' The American looked aghast. 'Now wait a minute,' he pleaded. 'Gimme a chance. I don't want this bundle of sticks on wheels. What would I do with it?'

'That's what I want you to tell me,' returned Biggles crisply. 'Come on, let's have the truth.'

'I wasn't doing any harm.'

'You were hoping to take this machine away. Why?'

'Oh, just to make some easy money, I guess,' muttered the American in a resigned voice.

'How? Come on, or you can answer questions somewhere else.'

'Listen,' said the American earnestly. 'If you pick me up for this I'm on a spot. I'm no crook.'

'What's your name?'

'Galton.'

'Where are you from?'

The American shrugged. 'Okay. I'll come clean. It wasn't my fault I couldn't buy the kite. I tried. You saw me. I'm a sergeant in the U.S. Air Force in Germany, supposed to be on pass in Berlin. Like a fool I got cleaned out in a gambling joint. There was a guy there named Silberman. He said he'd see me okay.'

'Why did he pick on you?'

'I was in uniform. I guess he could see I was a flyer.'

'You mean, he wanted you to do some flying for him in return for money?'

'Sure. That's it. All I had to do was come here and buy this old crate.'

'Did he say why he wanted it?'

'No. When I asked him he told me to quit asking questions. He gave me three hundred bucks to come over and buy the Crusader. Said that'd be enough. As you know it wasn't.'

'He didn't tell you he was wanted by the Federal Police, I'll warrant,' said Biggles grimly.

The American started. 'What for?'

'Treason.'

'The skunk. So that's why he was lying low in the Soviet Sector.'

'Never mind calling him names. Didn't it strike you as odd that he didn't come over here himself to buy the machine?'

'Sure it did. He said he couldn't come because he'd an important date in Berlin on the same day.'

'What were you to do with the machine when you got it?'

'I was to fly her to a place not far from here – Hookley Green. I suggested Hookley myself because I was stationed hereabouts for two years and know every inch of the country. Hookley was one of our practice landing grounds. There's plenty of room to get down and an old windmill makes a good landmark.'

'Is that all?'

'That's all, except he said someone would be at Hookley to take over the machine. He didn't say who, but the guy would pay me when I handed over.'

'He was taking a chance, wasn't he, trusting you with three hundred dollars?'

'Not likely,' said the American bitterly. 'He'd got me where he wanted me if I ratted on him. Oh, he's wise, that guy. You see, officially, I'm not allowed out of Berlin. To get me out he gave me forged papers. If I skipped with the money all he had to do was ring up my squadron, and then where would I be with a phoney pass? I must have been crazy to fall for this racket – but then, as I say, I was flat broke.'

'When were you to fly the machine to Hookley?'

'Right now. As soon as it got light.'

'Very well,' said Biggles in a business-like voice. 'Now let's see about getting this thing buttoned up. Silberman is an enemy of your country. Are you going to stick to him or are you coming in with us? I make no promise, but if you work with us I'll do my best to put things right with your commanding officer.'

'I'm with you,' answered Galton without hesitation. 'What do you want me to do?'

'Can you fly the Crusader?'

'Nothing to it. It's kid stuff after some of the crates I've had to handle.'

'Then give me an hour's start and fly it to Hookley as arranged. Can I trust you to do that?'

'You bet. I'll do anything if you'll get me out of this jam.'

'I'll be at Hookley when you get there,' promised Biggles.

As he made his way to the car, at the rear of the hangar, he whistled. A man appeared from the shadows. 'It's only Smithers,' he told the others. 'I told him to be around in case I needed him. He knows Silberman by sight.'

*

Leaving Galton with the Crusader they drove through narrow lanes to the spot where the aircraft was to be landed. It was flat, desolate country, and they could see the gaunt arms of the old windmill stark against the sky long before they reached it. In it, Biggles said, he expected Silberman would be waiting. There was nowhere else. He did not drive right up to it but stopped some distance away under cover of a line of willows. From there they went forward cautiously on foot to a point as near the windmill as could be reached without exposing themselves. Touching Biggles on the arm Ginger indicated another car parked close in behind the windmill. Biggles nodded.

A short wait followed. Then the lonely silence was broken by the sound for which they were prepared – the

rattle of an early type internal combustion engine. Into
sight, flying dangerously low, came the Crusader. With
mixed expressions of wonder and anxiety the watchers
followed it with their eyes as it skimmed the field. The
engine died suddenly. The nose dipped. The wheels
touched, bumped, and the aircraft, after bumping a
little way, finished on its nose not a score of paces from
where they crouched. Galton jumped down, and after a
whimsical grin at his gimcrack conveyance, lit a
cigarette.

By this time a man had left the windmill and was
hurrying towards him.

'Silberman,' whispered Smithers.

'So you made it?' cried Silberman delightedly, as he
reached his pilot.

'Sure I made it,' answered Galton.

Silberman wasted no time in further conversation.
With a knife in his hand he climbed into the open cockpit and worked on something too low for the watchers
to see, but it appeared to be either the floor or behind
the three-ply bulkhead. Presently he stood up, holding
in his hand a small roll. He then jumped down, almost
into the arms of Biggles, who taking advantage of the
man's preoccupation, had moved forward.

Silberman's expression would have been comical had
the circumstances been less dramatic.

'Is your name Joseph Silberman?' asked Biggles.

'Yes – why?'

Before the man could have realized fully what was
happening handcuffs had snapped on his wrists.

'I'll take that,' said Biggles, reaching for the roll and
handing it to Smithers who, opening it quickly, cried,
'It's the Flying Crusader!'

'I'm Detective Air Inspector Bigglesworth of Scotland Yard,' Biggles told his prisoner. 'I'm arresting you for stealing this picture from Mancroft Castle on a night in August, 1939. A more serious charge may be preferred later, so I must warn you that anything you say may be used as evidence against you.'

'Now don't be in a hurry,' choked Silberman, 'We can fix this between us. There's big money in it. When I was in Moscow I found –'

'Cut it,' requested Biggles curtly. 'You can tell your story later.' To Galton he said: 'You'd better get back to Berlin right away. I'll do what I can for you.'

The sequel, while remarkable, was not unexpected. The old legend was confirmed. Silberman confessed that he had come across a reference to the picture while, as a history student, he was going through the household accounts of the Tsar of the time it was painted. Following a clue contained in a simple cypher on the back of the picture, a panel was opened in the massive frame in which it had been shipped from Russia. In it was found a fortune in gems, the sale of which enabled Sir Giles to retain his ancient home and buy back the Flying Crusader, a silver replica of which now decorates the mantelpiece at Air Police Headquarters.

The honest Smithers, who had lost his life trying to defend his master's property, was avenged when Silberman went to the scaffold. His son, apart from the satisfaction of having cleared his father's name, did not go unrewarded, and is now a privileged person at Mancroft Castle, where the picture that was the cause of the trouble once more fills the frame from which it was cut.

5

THE MYSTERY OF
THE TORN PARACHUTE

BIGGLES looked at his chief inquiringly as he dropped into the chair beside the Air Commodore's desk at Special Air Police Headquarters in Scotland Yard. 'You said you had a question to ask me, sir,' he reminded.

The Air Commodore held up a piece of flimsy rag about a yard long and a foot wide, with tattered edges, and allowed it to sink softly on the desk. 'Animal, mineral or vegetable?' he asked.

'You've been watching television,' observed Biggles.

The Air Commodore smiled. 'Why not? Can you answer my question?'

Biggles took the rag, examined it closely and tested it for strength. 'If a silkworm is an animal then I'd say this is animal.'

'Correct. It is silk.'

'Judging from the quality, this line of stitching, and the gap where a shroud tore out, I'd say it's a fragment of parachute.'

'Correct again. It is.'

'It isn't British equipment.'

'You're doing fine.'

Biggles nodded sadly. 'And now I suppose you want me to tell you the name of the man who wore it – and tore it.'

'I'd very much like to know that.'

'Where did this rag come from, anyway?'

'It was found in the top of a tree in the Highlands of Scotland.'

Biggles stared. 'I see,' he said slowly. 'Then we can guess how it got there. No man in his right mind would climb a tree simply to hang out a piece of parachute fabric. It got hung up and tore off when the brolly was used.'

'That's how I'd worked it out. We have now arrived at the big question. Who used it?'

'Tell me all you know and I'll try another guess,' offered Biggles.

'That won't take long,' averred the Air Commodore. 'It started with a bird, known in the Highlands as the hoodie crow. It has some nasty habits, attacking newly-born lambs and young birds, for which reason farmers and gamekeepers wage war on it. The hoodie knows all about that, and has developed a cunning that makes it hard to approach. One of these birds decided to build its nest in a clump of Scots pines that stand on that desolate stretch of moorland between the River Spey and the Moray Firth. A gamekeeper saw what the bird was doing and decided to deal with it as murderers should be dealt with. During the hours of darkness before dawn he took up his position on its line of flight, well concealed, and waited for daybreak. But the bird was wise and didn't show up. Thinking it might be in the trees he started some careful stalking. He didn't see the crow, but we can judge his astonishment when he saw, high up on the end of a branch, a white object. His curiosity led him to climb the tree and this rag is what he found. He was all the more puzzled because he's prepared to swear it wasn't there the previous afternoon, when he tried to stalk the bird in daylight. Mystified, not knowing what the thing was, he asked the local police officer what he made of it. The officer, not knowing, asked his Superintendent, who, after some discreet inquiries, passed it on to us.'

'Did these inquiries throw any light on the mystery?'

'Only this. The gamekeeper says that as he sat there in the dark he heard a plane go over very high. It came from the south, appeared to circle once, and then made off in a north-easterly direction. He paid no attention to it, for there are several aerodromes on the north-east coast of Scotland and night flying is common.'

'Is that all?'

'All except that the keeper, knowing that the rag couldn't have got there by itself, and suspecting poachers, made a thorough examination of the ground for tracks. He found none.'

'Hm.' Biggles lit a cigarette. 'And I'm supposed to find out who used the parachute, and why.'

'That's your job. We can't have that sort of thing going on.'

Biggles looked pained. 'Have a heart, sir. I'm a policeman, not a magician.'

The Air Commodore's eyes twinkled. 'It's your business to keep the sky clean, so see what you can make of it.'

Biggles drew thoughtfully on his cigarette. 'It looks like a case of illegal entry into the country. Had it been an emergency drop the plane would have crashed. The fellow got away with it, too, for had he been killed or injured the keeper would have found him. You'll notice he chose a wide open space to drop into. Either he was lucky, or he knew the ground. He was clever to find the place in the dark, anyway – unless someone flashed a signal.'

'Those are the lines on which I was thinking. The jump was planned, not accidental.'

'There could be only one reason why a man should take such a risk. He didn't want to be seen at any ordinary point of entry, seaport or airport.' Biggles picked up a pencil and note-pad. 'When exactly did this happen?'

'On Tuesday, a fortnight ago today.'

'Any planes missing that night? I can't recall any.'

'There was none.'

'Any pilot or aircrew unaccounted for?'

'None. I've checked all those angles on the phone.'

'Did anyone outside aviation go missing at that time?'

'Three people. A man deserted from the army and hasn't been found. A civil servant absconded. He was tracked as far as Austria. A bank cashier named Lynsdale bolted with fifteen thousand pounds in used one pound notes. After the bank closed on the Saturday he flew to Paris, where he changed some English money into francs at a travel agency, and then booked on to Marseilles, where he bought a passage on a Portuguese tramp bound for the Far East.'

'And that's as much as you can tell me?'

'That's the lot.'

Biggles got up. 'All right, sir. I'll see what I can make of it. One or two points occur to me. I'll follow them up and see if they lead to a tree-top in Morayshire.'

*

Biggles walked back to his own office where Ginger was waiting, Algy and Bertie being on leave.

'What's the drill?' inquired Ginger.

'Quite simple,' answered Biggles cynically. 'A fortnight ago somebody jumped out of an aircraft, with a brolly, and touched down in Morayshire. We've got to find out who it was.'

'Is that all?' asked Ginger, with biting sarcasm.

'It should be enough to keep us busy for a day or two,' returned Biggles evenly. 'If you'll listen I'll tell you about it.' During the next ten minutes he passed on the information provided by the Air Commodore.

'Any ideas?' asked Ginger, when he had finished.

'Yes, but they're a bit thin,' replied Biggles, throwing the fragment of parachute on the table. 'That brolly wasn't made in this country. It's pure silk, reinforced. As it came from abroad we may suppose the aircraft also came from abroad. France and Italy use silk. We'll start with France. Get me Marcel Brissac, at the Interpol office in Paris, on the phone – on the private line if it's disengaged.'

Within three minutes Ginger was handing him the telephone. 'Marcel on the line,' he said.

The conversation that followed occupied some time, and when Biggles hung up there was a pensive expression on his face. 'That may turn out to be a lucky shot, even if it's off the particular mark we're shooting at. Marcel says he was going to speak to me anyway. Here's the thing in a nutshell. He's got a machine missing: a Loire four-seater out on a charter job; Le

Bourget to Liverpool. The point is, the passenger was an Englishman – fellow named Norman Harrington White. I smell something fishy there.'

'Why?'

'Naturally, he had to pay for the trip in advance, in cash. Seventy-five thousand francs; which is about seventy-five pounds. How did he get all that money? The basic allowance granted in this country for travel to France is considerably less.'

'What reason did he give for such a trip?'

'He said it was vital that he caught a ship due to sail from Liverpool at dawn, for Buenos Aires.'

'Which means it was a night flight.'

'The plane left the ground, fuelled for the return trip, just after midnight. That was a fortnight ago today. It hasn't been seen since. But wait a minute. White, who said he'd never been in the air before, was desperately nervous, and asked if he could have a parachute. There was no reason why he shouldn't. After all, he was the customer; so they lent him one. I suppose such a thing could happen, but it's a bit unusual. The fact emerges, a French aircraft, carrying a French parachute, flew to England on the night that a piece of torn French parachute was found in northern Scotland. Is that a coincidence – or what is it?'

'But Liverpool's a long step from Morayshire.'

'The plane never arrived at Liverpool. The pilot spoke to three airfields after crossing the coast. It was then dead on course. After that there wasn't another peep. Marcel's inquiries have established that, and there the trail ends. What happened to the aircraft? Had it crashed on land the wreck would have been found by now. As it was a clear night one can't imagine an experienced pilot losing himself over the sea.'

'If, as Marcel says, the aircraft carried enough fuel for the return flight, it *could* have reached Scotland.'

'It could,' agreed Biggles. 'But we'll come back to that in a minute. As far as Marcel knows, with this exception, no French aircraft other than regular services were over England that night. No passenger has been reported missing. Air liners don't carry parachutes, anyway. Of course, it's possible that there might be two machines over England at the same time, both carrying French parachutes; but that it should happen at the same hour, on the same night, that one of them was used, would be stretching coincidence to the limit. I shall, therefore, rule it out – for the time being, at any rate.'

'You mean, you will assume that there was only one machine.'

'Yes. And if we're right, that machine, however improbable it may seem, went to Scotland. Now let's try a spot of elimination. It could have got there only in one of three ways. The pilot flew it. The passenger flew it. It flew itself. It *might* have flown itself: but that presupposes that the two people in it were dead or unconscious – which they were not, for one of them jumped out. That leaves us with the pilot and his passenger. Can you think of any possible reason why an experienced pilot, starting for Liverpool in good weather conditions, should find himself in the north of Scotland?'

'No.'

'Neither can I,' went on Biggles. 'Even if the passenger said he'd changed his mind and had decided to go to Inverness instead, would the pilot have flown on? He would not. He had been paid to go to Liverpool. His chart, his compass course – everything, would have been prepared for Liverpool. Allowing for the remote possibility that the pilot *did* agree to change his course, he would certainly have notified ground stations. Moreover, he would have known his passenger was up to some funny business, for the alleged purpose of the flight was to catch a ship at Liverpool.'

'Okay,' agreed Ginger. 'That leaves us with a passenger who had never before been in the air.'

'Who *said* he'd never been in the air? There's a lot of difference.'

'You're suggesting he was a liar.'

'I'm suspicious of him. His reason for wanting a brolly is unconvincing. Would any ordinary man, however nervous he might be, admit funk in front of other men? I don't think so. And how did he get all those francs? We can soon check up on that. Ring the Bank of England, Foreign Currency Branch, give our code number and ask if a man named Norman Harrington White, has, within the last few weeks, been granted an overseas allowance, and if so, how much.'

Ginger went to the phone and put through the inquiry. 'The Bank has no record of anyone of that name,' he reported presently, hanging up.

'We're getting on,' remarked Biggles. 'We know now that Mr. White had no authority to be in France. In those circumstances he would hardly be likely to present himself to the officials at any airport in this country. If he did he would have to show his passport; and a passport shows how much money one is entitled to take out of the country. In this case it was none. Of course, the name on the passport might not have been White; but that would make no difference; the Currency Control people would still want to know how he got seventy-five thousand francs. We can now take it that White never had the slightest intention of going to Liverpool.'

'Okay,' agreed Ginger. 'So White was phoney. Where *was* he going?'

'I don't know; but it looks as if he intended to keep clear of Customs airports. A licensed pilot wouldn't risk his ticket or his machine, much less his neck, by landing anywhere else. How otherwise could White get down? There's only one way. By parachute.'

'He might have arranged with the pilot to let him jump,' suggested Ginger.

'In which case the pilot would then have returned home. The machine didn't get home. Why? Obviously, because something had happened to prevent it.'

'You think White intended from the start to go to Scotland?'

'It begins to look like that,' averred Biggles. 'We know that district where this piece of rag was found. It's ideal for a jump. There isn't a house, much less a village, for some miles. It's mostly open moor with a little natural timber here and there. Was it by pure chance that the man dropped there, or did he know it? It so happened that the brolly fouled a tree. Proceeding along this line of surmise we must ask ourselves, what did he do next? Where did he go? He certainly went somewhere. As he was obviously working on a carefully prepared plan we can assume that he had an objective. How did he intend to reach it? Roads and railways being few and far between he would in any case have to walk some distance to reach transport of any kind.'

'Having gone to so much trouble to get to Scotland he may have stayed there.'

'All right. But there's a lot of room in Scotland. Did he stay in the district or did he go somewhere else? Did he walk to the nearest railway-station or had he arranged for road transport? No public services would be operating at the hour he must have jumped. But we shan't answer these questions sitting here, so let's slip up in the Proctor and see what we can make of it on the spot.'

*

Three hours later, the police Proctor, at five thousand feet, heading for Dalcross airfield, was over the wide, rolling, heather-clad wastes, dotted with an occasional stand of pines, that lie between the Spey and the Moray Firth. The river, winding through its broad strath with the little Speyside railway that keeps it company, was below. Filling the distant horizon ahead was the sea.

'It must have been in one of those clumps of trees down there that the keeper found the rag,' observed Biggles. 'The nearest road – in fact, the only road – is the one that crosses the open moor from Forres, up north, to that village beside the river. What's the name of it?'

Ginger, who was sitting with the map on his knees, answered: 'Knockando. There's a railway-station there.'

'The man who parachuted down here must have made for that road, no matter whether he intended going to the station or to look for motor transport. By the time he got to it, it would be daylight, so somebody must have seen him. In lonely country like this a stranger is soon spotted. We'll get a car at Forres and come back over the ground.'

'Are you going to call on the keeper?' asked Ginger.

'I don't think so. He's already told all he knows. I

want to find out, if possible, how our parachutist left the district.'

Biggles landed at Dalcross. An airport car took them to Forres, from where, in a hired car, they returned to the wide open spaces which they had surveyed from the air. 'It'd be hard to find a more ideal spot for a para-chute jump,' remarked Biggles. 'Look at this road. Not a house or a tree for miles. I still suspect our unknown visitor chose it deliberately.'

'Which means that he must have had some knowledge of it.'

'Of course.'

Biggles drove straight to the little Speyside station of Knockando. The station-master, who was porter, book-ing-clerk and everything else, was there. Biggles, in-troducing himself as a railway inspector checking tickets, asked the man if he recalled selling a ticket to a stranger on the first train on the vital Tuesday. The answer was no. In fact, the station agent said he hadn't sold a ticket to anyone. He hadn't seen a stranger. He knew everyone up and down Speyside, and had there been a visitor about he would have heard of it. Indeed, the man was so emphatic that Biggles regarded him with mild as-tonishment. 'I see you take an interest in strangers,' he remarked.

'Aye, and guid reason,' was the curt reply.

As they went back to the car Ginger smiled, realizing that they themselves were strangers. 'I wonder what he meant by that,' he said.

Biggles shrugged. 'It seems our parachutist didn't go by train.'

'He might have gone to another station.'

'Why should he walk several miles? It wasn't necessary. Once on the ground, he must have felt safe. No. Had he intended to go by train he would have made for the nearest station. If he didn't go by train he must have used a car. There's nothing else. That's assuming he left the district. Let's go and have a word with the policeman.'

They found the constable just in from his round. He had seen no one he did not know, either on the night of the landing or afterwards. He seemed to share the railway man's suspicions of strangers; so much so that Biggles' curiosity prompted him to ask why.

'Maybe you London fellers think people like me have an easy time of it here,' was the answer. 'Well, we don't. We work day and night. What with people breaking into the distilleries for whisky, gangs netting the river for salmon or poaching the deer, we have to keep our eyes open for strangers, and for strange cars.'

'Have you seen a strange car lately?' asked Biggles quickly.

'No. But if you want to know about cars go and see Captain Mackenzie.'

'Who's he?'

'He's in charge of the river watchers here for the Spey Fishery Board. Gangs come from as far afield as Glasgow these days, to net the salmon. No car gets in and out of this area at night without its number being taken. Motor cycle bailies keep an eye on strangers.'

'That's useful,' said Biggles. 'Where does Captain Mackenzie live?'

'The Grey House, on the Grantown Road.'

'Thanks,' returned Biggles. 'We'll go and have a word with him.'

In half an hour they were with the Fishery Board official.

T—E

'Yes, cars are my headache,' he told them. 'There's no other way for poachers to get about with their nets, and carry home perhaps twenty or thirty fish. It's the cars we look for. We check everyone in and out of this area at night. Of course, my watchers, who are posted with motor cycles at strategic points, know all the local vehicles.'

'Could you tell me what cars were on the roads between three a.m. and seven, a week last Tuesday?' asked Biggles.

'Easily.' The official reached for his records. 'There were four,' he announced. 'Gordon's van went through from Elgin. Pickfords went through to Grantown. Only cars. Smith – he's one of our local farmers, crossed the bridge; on his way to the sheep sale at Perth, I suppose. The other was Mrs. Williams. Her Austin went out just after two in the Forres direction and came back a little before five.'

'Is she local?'

'Yes. Englishwoman. Lives on Strathspey, near Tomindalloch. Took Dalglennie House about two months ago. Nice young woman. Drove her car up from London.' The official smiled. 'She's not likely to worry me,' he concluded, his mind apparently still running on his job, which was the prevention of salmon poaching.

'Has this lady a family?'

'I don't think so. She's a widow, I believe, and as far as I know she lives alone.'

'I see,' said Biggles, getting up. 'Well, thank you very much, Captain Mackenzie. You've been most helpful.'

'That seems to settle the car question,' remarked Ginger, when they were outside.

'I'm not so sure of that,' replied Biggles, as he drove

off. 'Two in the morning seems a funny time for a young woman, living alone, to go out. What could she have been doing on that lonely road to Forres? We'll go and have a look at this house, Dalglennie. We may be wasting our time, but I'm more than ever convinced that the man who jumped out of that aircraft had transport of some sort. Mrs. Williams' car was apparently the only one on the Forres road at the critical time. In fact, it was the only car out in this district without a reasonable purpose. We might as well probe all the possibilities while we're here. This village we're coming to must be Tomindalloch. Hello! there's an Austin – outside the grocer's. London registration. Could be Mrs. Williams doing her shopping. We'll see.'

Biggles pulled up outside the shop, which, like many village shops, was also the post office. Leaving the car they went in to find a good-looking young woman giving her grocery order. They turned over some miscellaneous newspapers until it was completed when the shopkeeper wished the lady a polite 'Good morning, Mrs. Williams.'

As the woman went out Biggles faced the man. 'We're from London,' he announced. 'As you may have heard, a number of mail-bags have lately been stolen and we're checking up on registered parcels in this district. There was one I believe for a Mrs. Williams about a fortnight ago. Was it delivered?'

'That's the lady who's just gone out,' volunteered the shopkeeper. 'Yes, she got the parcel all right. I can tell you that without looking at my book. She happened to be in the shop when the London mail came in, so she took it with her.'

'Good,' returned Biggles. 'Thank you. That's all I wanted to know. Good morning.'

As they got back into the car Biggles was smiling faintly.

'Judging from the quantity of groceries the lady was buying she seems to have a healthy appetite,' he remarked. 'Her name must be Williams, anyhow. Let's see where she lives. She went this way.'

'You seem particularly interested in her.'

'I'm more interested in the car, since it's the only one that came across the Forres road on the night, and at about the same time, that somebody arrived by air.'

A drive of a mile took them to the house, a well-built cottage standing in a pleasant garden a little way back from the road. The name was on the gate. The Austin stood by the front door. Biggles drove past and allowed the car to run to a stop in the deep shade of some trees a short distance beyond. Watching the house he lit a cigarette. Presently the woman they had seen in the shop came out and started unloading from the Austin the groceries she had bought. In this she was joined by a man, dressed in old tweeds, who walked with a pronounced limp. A stubble of beard covered his chin.

'Seems that the lady doesn't live alone after all,' observed Biggles dryly. 'I thought she was buying a lot of food for one.' He looked at his watch. 'Time's getting on. We'd better head back for Forres or we'll be late for the evening meal.'

'And then what?' asked Ginger.

'We'll waffle back to London in the morning and see what news they have there,' decided Biggles.

*

It was nearly noon the following day when, back at Scotland Yard, on their way to Headquarters, Biggles knocked on the door of Inspector Gaskin's office and walked in.

'Don't bring any more bad news to me,' growled the Inspector. 'I've plenty to go on with.'

'Shan't keep you long,' promised Biggles, soothingly. 'The Air Commodore was telling me about a London bank cashier named Lynsdale bolting with fifteen thousand of the best.'

The Inspector glowered. 'All right. Don't rub it in.'

'I take it you haven't found him?'

'Lost him at Marseilles. He's at the other side of the world by now. He had it all nicely planned.'

'The queer thing is,' said Biggles evenly, 'no matter how well a job is planned, something usually gets torn to let the cat out of the bag.'

'Nothing got torn in this case,' stated the Inspector shortly.

'Oh, yes it did.'

'What?'

'This.' Biggles tossed the piece of fabric on the desk. 'Tell me,' he went on, 'is that the Lynsdale file on your desk?'

'It is. And I'm sick of looking at it.'

'Did he by chance associate with a woman named Mrs. Williams?'

'Yes. Sister. A widow. She used to keep house for him.'

'Left him a couple of months ago. Am I right?'

The Inspector's eyes opened wide. 'How did *you* know?'

Biggles ignored the question. 'Was Lynsdale ever in the R.A.F.?'

'He was.'

'Served on one of the airfields in north-east Scotland, perhaps.'

'Dalcross. Bomber pilot. Who told you all this?'

Biggles smiled. 'A little bird. Would I be right in saying he walks with a limp?'

'Broke a thigh in a crash and was invalided out. You've been looking at this file!'

'Better still, I've been looking at Lynsdale,' stated Biggles, his smile broadening at the expression on the Inspector's face. 'He's growing a beard, so you may find him changed a bit.'

'Do you mean he didn't sail on that Portuguese ship from Marseilles?'

'I don't see how he could have done. At the moment he's living with his sister at a nice little place in Morayshire called Dalglennie House, near Tomindalloch. I fancy you'll find the missing notes there.' Biggles held up the parachute fabric. 'Also the rest of this.'

'What is it?'

'The thing that got torn to let the cat out of the bag. Let me have it back for my collection of criminal curiosities when you've finished with it. So long.'

Leaving the Inspector looking dazed they went on to Headquarters.

'Well?' greeted the Air Commodore, smiling. 'Did you find our mysterious night-bird?'

'Yes,' answered Biggles inconsequentially.

The Air Commodore's expression of gentle banter switched to one of amazement. 'You did?' he ejaculated.

Biggles nodded.

'Who was it?'

'Lynsdale, the missing cashier.'

'How on earth did you work that out?'

'No trouble at all,' replied Biggles, pulling up a chair. 'Strange how so often the most difficult-looking jobs turn out to be the easiest. Lynsdale made a plan that must have looked fool-proof, but he made one fundamental error – one that anybody could have made. He assumed – as indeed we did – that the district into which he proposed to jump was perfect for the job. Actually, he couldn't have chosen a worse place. Anywhere else and I doubt if a piece of rag in a tree would have attracted attention. Admittedly that was an accident; but in a thinly populated district where anything in the slightest degree unusual excites curiosity, it was fatal. To look down on those lonely moors from above, as Lynsdale had, one might suppose them to be asleep. On the contrary, they're very much alert. Salmon and deer poaching is now big business, with the result that strangers are regarded with suspicion and cars moving about at night come under closer observation than would be possible in an urban district.' Biggles reached for a cigarette.

'From the start I thought there was something fishy about Lynsdale's effort,' he went on. 'That trail he left to Marseilles was a bit *too* easy to follow. Why change notes at a travel agency where a record would be kept? How did he get a big bundle of notes through Customs? Actually, he had more sense than to try. Keeping only enough for his immediate purpose he posted the rest to his sister, in Scotland, who was waiting for them to arrive. He then blazed a trail to Marseilles and doubled back to Paris, homeward bound. Naturally, he daren't show his passport anywhere; but he had it all arranged. As he was able to fly, all he needed was an aircraft and a parachute to get where he wanted to go. Having chartered a plane in the name of White he had to get rid of it, and the pilot. Somewhere over the Midlands he must have knocked the unlucky pilot on the head and gone on to Scotland. Having got to his objective, where his sister was waiting with a car, all he had to do was turn the nose of the machine towards the North Sea, set the controls for level flight, and step overboard with his brolly. The aircraft, running out of fuel, would crash in the sea and disappear without trace. A clever but dastardly piece of cold-blooded murder. His sister had got the new home ready, and there, no doubt, they reckoned to live in comfort without any more money troubles. That's all. I've told Gaskin.'

'In which case they won't live in comfort much longer,' said the Air Commodore grimly. 'Good show. You deserve a lunch for that. Let's go round to the club.'

6

THE CASE OF THE
MISSING CONSTABLE

BIGGLES was scanning the daily batch of aviation press cuttings as Ginger handed them to him, in the Scotland Yard office of the Special Air Police, when Inspector Gaskin walked in.

'Morning, Inspector, how's life?' greeted Biggles cheerfully, without stopping what he was doing.

'Grim,' replied the Inspector gloomily, sinking into a chair and thumbing his pipe.

'What's on your mind?'

'Oh, it's this missing policeman affair. The newspapers have started the usual scream about inefficiency. What do they think we are – conjurers? The *Daily Courier* has offered a thousand pounds for the body, dead or alive – as if that'll help.'

'They don't seriously expect it to help. A reward keeps public interest alive, and the police on their toes, which is good for everybody. Be a joke if someone knocked 'em for a thousand! If it was in my line I'd have a crack at it.'

'That's what I was thinking. Since you've been at the Yard you've developed a knack of spotting something the rest of us miss.'

'I've only glanced at the case. There's no air angle to it, is there?'

'There's just a chance there might be, although I'll admit I can't see how. A plane has been in the habit of landing near the place where the officer must have disappeared.'

'By night?'

'No. Only by day.'

'You've got the gen on this aircraft, I suppose?'

'Yes. Seems straightforward enough. Bloke drops in to see his brother. Lands on a twenty-acre field next to the churchyard. I can't find any hook-up with our case.'

'Tell me about it.'

The Inspector lit his pipe. 'The missing man is Edward Small, who for the last two years has had charge of the village of Elmthorpe, in Hertfordshire. Young chap. Place is only a hamlet. Until recently Small lived with his mother in a cottage in the main street. Three weeks ago she died, and was buried in the local churchyard. He was upset, naturally, but not to the point of doing anything silly. Since then he's had a daily woman looking after him. On Friday the fourteenth – that was five days after his mother died – Small was due for night duty round his beat – a matter of four miles. The beat starts at one end of the village, makes a circle, and comes back in the other end. In addition to the village it takes in one or two farms, labourers' cottages, the rectory, the churchyard and some lands belonging to the church, which includes the twenty-acre pasture I mentioned just now. There's a second-class road all the way.

'Small had his supper late, about ten-thirty, after seeing the people out of the pub at closing time. He was perfectly normal then. It was a fine, warm summer night.

Telling his woman the arrangements for the following day he put on his helmet and went out. From that moment no one has set eyes on him. He was to have met an officer from Stevenage half-way, but he didn't turn up, so we can reckon that whatever happened to him occurred on the first half of the beat.'

'I take it this is a rural district?' queried Biggles.

'As rural as anywhere in the land.'

'What about poachers?'

'Hasn't been a case of poaching for years.'

'Any other crime in the district?'

'Not actually in the village. There have been some burglaries in the big country houses round about; but that's happening everywhere. Matter of fact there was a neat job done at Clagston Hall the night Small disappeared; but we needn't bring that in because the nearest point of Small's beat to Clagston Hall is close on six miles. He couldn't have been near the place. Anyway, the burglary wasn't discovered until long after he should have been home.'

'Have you got a line on this burglar?'

'No. But all these jobs were the work of the same man. Same method. He seems to know his way about. Gets in through an upstairs bathroom window. Takes nothing but cash and jewellery. Must carry his own ladder. Never touches those belonging to the house. Must be a new hand at the game, because although I've a good set of fingerprints we've no record of them at the Yard.'

'Sounds like an inside job.'

'You'd think that; but I've been through the households with a tooth-comb, for no result. Caused a fuss by even taking fingerprints of the staff.'

Biggles nodded. 'Well, he's your headache. Tell me about this plane.'

'It belongs to the rector's brother. I called on the parson and asked him about it. He's an amiable sort of chap, named Dewsberry, about forty, unmarried. Lives at the rectory with a housekeeper. He's been there twelve years and seems popular with everybody, high and low. He told me his brother was a flying instructor at Dacton Aero Club, in Yorkshire. Flies down occasionally to see him, landing in the big field next to the churchyard. It belongs to the rectory, so there's no difficulty about that.'

'Why does he *fly* down?'

'Apparently it's a day's journey by train. By air it can be done in an hour. Sounded reasonable to me.'

Biggles lit a cigarette. 'May be. But the Air Ministry now frowns on these casual landings outside official airports. So do I, if it comes to that. They're dangerous. And besides, as we know, such landings facilitate illegal practices – Customs evasions, currency rackets, and so on.'

'Well, I'm not suggesting that there's anything like that in this case. But a plane *has* landed at Elmthorpe. I may be clutching at straws, but there seemed a vague chance that it might come into the picture, which is why I looked in to see you. As a matter of detail the plane hasn't been down for over a month. I confirmed that in the village.'

'As that was before Small disappeared it's hard to see how it could be involved. However, let's check.' Biggles turned to Ginger. 'Give me the Dacton Club file.'

The file was put on the table. Biggles went through it. 'Here we are. Chief Instructor, Richard Ernest

Dewsberry. That must be the man. Hello, what's this? Licence suspended for twelve months and fined fifty pounds for failing to declare a quantity of saccharin on entry into the country from France. That was three years ago. Not very nice for his brother, being a parson. I wonder where he is now. Ginger, put a call through to the club secretary.' Biggles turned back to the Inspector. 'Do you seriously want me to go on with this?'

'It couldn't do any harm. I've explored every angle and I still haven't a clue.'

'There's usually one; the trouble is to find it. No matter. It's a fine day for a stroll in the country. I'll go and have a look at Elmthorpe.'

'Fly down?'

'No. It isn't worth it. We don't want a police plane seen in the vicinity, anyway. I'll take the car.'

'Do you want me to come with you? I know my way around.'

Biggles smiled. 'Which means that everyone in the village must know who you are and what you're doing. No thanks. A couple of casual visitors should pass without comment.'

'Just as you like,' agreed Gaskin, getting up. 'You might as well have my map. You'll find everything marked on it.'

Ginger came over from the 'phone. 'Nothing doing,' he reported. 'I spoke to the steward. The secretary is away on holiday and Dewsberry has been abroad for three weeks conducting a tour of club members across Europe.'

The Inspector shrugged. 'That settles any argument about him. If he was on the Continent the night Small disappeared, obviously he wasn't at Elmthorpe.'

'It would seem like that,' agreed Biggles. 'Get the car round, Ginger. We'll have a look at this field.' He smiled. 'If we *could* make the *Courier* cough up a thousand pounds it'd teach them to have more respect for the police.'

'That'd be lovely,' agreed Gaskin, grinning. 'Have a go at it.'

*

Rather less than two hours later Ginger stopped the car on the road beside the gate that gave access to the rectory acre field. They got out, Biggles, with the Inspector's map, which he had been studying on the way down, in his hand. For a minute they gazed in silence. Then Biggles said: 'Well, what do you make of it?'

Ginger's eyes went to some tall trees rising from the hedge on their side of the field, and more opposite. Towards the village end a church steeple rose above still more trees. 'Not too good,' he opined. 'I expected a square field, not a long narrow one. With a north-east wind blowing a landing would be easy enough because you would come in low with the length of the field in front of you. From any other direction you'd be taking a chance with the trees. Dewsberry, being an Instructor, might risk it.'

'If he had a reason.'

'What do you mean by that?'

'Well, I've done a fair amount of flying, but I wouldn't take a chance on landing here – unless the wind was dead right – merely to make a social call. The fact that Dewsberry is an experienced pilot would make him hesitate, too – unless he's a fool.'

'I see what you mean,' returned Ginger slowly.

'Anything else strike you?'

'No.' Ginger gave Biggles a second glance. 'Now what are you thinking?'

'There's one thing that strikes me as odd. In the ordinary way one wouldn't notice it. But this isn't an ordinary occasion. I came here in a suspicious mood, looking for anything in the slightest degree unusual. Here we have a nice field of grass. With agriculture on its toes with food production, why are no sheep or cattle taking advantage of all this feed? It's worth money. It belongs to the rectory. The rector's stipend can't be all that big that he needn't bother to increase it by letting this grazing to a farmer. I can think of one reason for that. With sheep or cattle roaming about a plane wouldn't be able to land. It follows, therefore – if my guess is right – that the rector keeps the field clear so that his brother can land.'

'What's wrong with that?'

'Nothing, except that I got quite a different impression from Gaskin, who was given to understand that these landings were merely a matter of a fellow dropping in to have a word with his brother. We now have a different picture. Dewsberry, the pilot, is apparently prepared to take risks in order to land. And his brother, the rector, is willing to chuck away a hundred pounds a year in order to say "hello" to him. It looks to me as if they have a definite reason for meeting. Of course, all this may add up to nothing, but we came here to study the air angle and look for something Gaskin missed. He knows his job, so if we're to find anything new we've got to dig deep and examine every detail, however trifling.'

'Dewsberry may only fly down when the wind is right for a safe landing.'

'Living in the north of England how would he know the direction of the wind here?'

'He might ring up and find out.'

'That supports my argument that these meetings are arranged, and not just casual affairs. But let's go along to the village pub, park the car and see if we can get something to eat.'

'Just a minute,' said Ginger quickly. 'There's the parson now, coming over the stile from the churchyard.'

'What's he doing?'

A black-clad figure was now in the field. With head bowed and hands folded behind him he was walking slowly towards the gate by which they stood.

'He seems deep in thought,' observed Ginger.

'The field's his own property, so there's no reason why he shouldn't take a stroll across it if he feels like it,' Biggles pointed out.

'He looks as if he might be mushrooming.'

'It's too early for mushrooms. Looking to see how much grass he's got, maybe. Let's pretend to be doing something to the car. We don't want him to think we're snooping.'

The clergyman came on, without raising his eyes, to the gate, where he subjected the ground to a close scrutiny. He then turned about, and taking a slightly different course, returned to the churchyard.

'He's lost something,' decided Ginger.

'That's what it looks like,' agreed Biggles. 'Let's press on to the tavern.'

They managed to get a simple meal, but learned nothing of the mystery that had brought them to the village. Biggles refrained from asking questions for fear the landlord might guess their purpose and spread the news.

Lunch over, they went out, and leaving the car sauntered down the street. 'Now,' said Biggles quietly, when they came to the home of the missing officer, 'this is where Police Constable Small started on the night he disappeared. We'll follow in his footsteps, or the steps we might suppose he would take in the ordinary course of his duties. But between here and a point on his beat something extraordinary must have happened. There's just a chance, if we use our heads and our eyes, we might get a line on what that was. Gaskin has been over the ground before us, but I still feel it would be a mystery indeed if a full-grown man could be spirited away without leaving a trace behind him. There's not a shred of evidence to suggest that he went voluntarily. In fact, everything points the other way, which means that there must have been violence.'

They set off.

Their route took them out of the bottom end of the village, with occasional houses on either side, the occupants of which must have heard any sounds of an unusual nature on the night of the constable's disappearance. For a quarter of a mile the road then ran straight between thick-set hedges, without a turning on either side, to the gravel drive that led through an avenue of trees to the rectory. To the right was the low stone wall that bounded the churchyard with its many tombstones, and the grey pile of the church beyond.

Biggles paused at the drive. 'We can't very well go up there without being observed by the parson or his housekeeper, and I'd rather that didn't happen – yet.' He went on to the open lychgate from which a path curved to the church porch.

Ginger would have walked past, but Biggles stopped. 'I said we'd follow Small's probable footsteps,' he remarked.

'But would he go into the churchyard?' queried Ginger, looking surprised.

'If your mother had been buried there five days ago would you walk straight past?'

'No.'

'What would you do?'

'I'd stop and think about her. With the grave so close I might walk in and have a look at it.'

'I'm pretty sure you would. So would anybody. Small thought a lot of his mother, don't forget. In fact, if there's any place on his beat where he had reason to stop, it's here.' Biggles walked up the path between the last resting places of bygone generations of villagers.

They had no difficulty in finding the grave of Mrs. Small, even though it was tucked away in a corner near the stile that gave access to the big field, for the newly turned earth was conspicuous, as were some simple wreaths of flowers, now withered. An ancient yew with low-hanging branches kept silent guard. Under it was the stump of another, to form a convenient seat of which Biggles took advantage.

'The next question is, assuming that Small came here, how long did he stay?' he said lighting a cigarette, and flicking the match away. In a moment he had stooped and picked up something from the mossy grass near where the match had fallen. It was a cigarette end. 'It looks as if he might have sat here long enough to smoke a cigarette,' he said quietly, answering his own question.

'Anyone might have smoked that,' Ginger pointed out.

'Agreed. But who more likely than the man whose mother lies buried a few feet away? There are more comfortable seats than this for anyone without an interest in this particular spot.' Biggles searched the ground, and was rewarded by another cigarette end and two dead matches. 'Somebody sat here long enough to smoke two cigarettes,' he affirmed. 'It could have been Small. There would be nothing remarkable about that.'

'But what could have happened to him here, of all places?'

Biggles shrugged. 'You could say that of anywhere on his beat. But something certainly did happen to him, somewhere.' He got up, and walking to the grave, gazed at it thoughtfully. Presently he went on, in a curious voice: 'Something, I don't know what, but *something* has happened here.'

'What makes you think that?'

'Because flowers are put on a grave after it has been filled in, not before.' Stooping, Biggles took a stalk that protruded from the loose earth and drew out a crushed carnation.

'That certainly is a bit odd,' muttered Ginger. 'Here's another. What vandal would trample on a grave?'

'That's what we would like to know,' answered Biggles softly. 'Not Small – at any rate, not deliberately.'

'Here's a piece of black ribbon half buried – off one of the cards, I imagine.' Taking between his finger and thumb the ribbon that had been exposed by the removal of the flower, Ginger pulled. About six inches of ribbon came to light, and then a larger piece of material, also black, to which it was attached. There were two oval-shaped holes in it, and Ginger caught his breath when he realized what he held. In the circumstances it would have been difficult to imagine anything more sinister.

It was a mask.

'Put it out of sight – quickly,' snapped Biggles. 'We may be watched.'

Ginger noticed that even he had turned pale.

'Come over here,' went on Biggles, in a curious voice, going back to the tree. 'Now we *have* got something to think about,' he added.

Silence fell. From the shade of the yew his eyes surveyed the churchyard, mellow in warm summer sunshine. Rooks drifted in and out of the steeple.

After a while he resumed, musingly. 'The last person buried in this churchyard was Mrs. Small. Had there been another death in the village we should see the grave. That little grey stone building in the corner must be where the sexton keeps his stuff. If he hasn't had another grave to dig it probably hasn't been used since Mrs. Small died. I wonder could he tell us anything? I think I'll have a word with him.'

Biggles thought again for a minute or two and then moved as if he had made up his mind. 'Look, Ginger,' he said crisply. 'I'm going back to the village to ask one or two questions. I want you to go to the Yard, find Gaskin and bring him here right away. Tell him to bring his best fingerprint man, with his equipment. Say I'd like to see the case file on the local burglaries. Oh, yes, and he might bring a bunch of skeleton keys. That's all. Be as quick as you can. You'll find me waiting by the grave.'

'Okay,' agreed Ginger.

They walked back to the road by way of the sexton's

shed. Biggles took a glance through the window in passing, but said nothing.

At the lychgate they turned towards the village, and the car.

*

The glow of sunset was fading behind the elms that gave the village its name when Ginger, after parking the car near the lychgate, led the way through the silent churchyard to the stump where Biggles waited. With him were Inspector Gaskin, carrying a brief-case, and Tomkins of the fingerprint department, with his bag of equipment.

'What's all this about?' demanded Gaskin, looking hard at Biggles.

'Ginger told you what we found here?'

'Yes. What do you make of it?'

'Sit down and I'll tell you,' answered Biggles. 'Talk quietly. I've an idea. I may be wrong, But if I'm right I'd rather you dealt with it than me.'

'Was I right about the plane coming into the picture?'

'Yes and no,' replied Biggles vaguely. 'We'll come to that presently. Have you brought all the things I asked for?'

'Yes.'

'Good. Then let's get busy. I want Tomkins to check the handle of that shed over there for fingerprints. He'll need the keys, because I then want him to go inside and check the handle of the spade that hangs on the wall. There will certainly be plenty of fingerprints on that. Better take photos. We may need them for evidence. In fact, he'd better bring the spade back with him. Carry on, Tomkins.'

'Are you pulling my leg?' asked Gaskin, with a touch of asperity as Tomkins went off.

'I am not,' returned Biggles shortly. 'This is neither the time nor the place for jokes.'

For ten minutes they sat and watched the flashes of Tomkins' photographic equipment. Then he returned.

'We'll now go into the church,' said Biggles, rising.

'The church!' exclaimed Gaskin. 'What in thunder has the church got to do with it?'

'This,' replied Biggles succinctly. 'Whatever finger-prints Tomkins may have found on the handle of the shed, or on the spade, will tell us nothing, because we shan't know who made them. But if we go into the church, and take some prints from the front of the pulpit, we may get an idea.'

'Are you talking about the parson?' cried Gaskin incredulously.

'Only one man goes into the pulpit; so if the prints we find there are the same as those on the door handle, and the spade, we shall know who made them all, shan't we?' stated Biggles evenly. 'You see, since Ginger went to fetch you I've been to the village and spoken to the sexton. He's a part-time man – digs the graves and tolls the bell on Sundays. He hasn't been into that shed, or used the spade, since Mrs. Small died. His fingerprints, therefore, should be on them. The same prints should also be on the key of the shed, which, he tells me, hangs on a nail just inside the front door of the rectory, where he can get it when he wants it. If they're not, we shall know someone else has used it.'

'Who else would want it?'

'I can think of no one but the parson. Come on.'

Biggles walked over to the massive door of the church. 'Open up,' he told Tomkins.

The skeleton keys jangled as several were tried: then the door, with a creak of hinges, swung open. Biggles walked down the gloomy aisle. 'Go ahead,' he told Tomkins. 'You know what I want you to do.'

After the warm air outside the interior of the old stone building struck chill; but the chill that ran down Ginger's spine was not entirely due to atmosphere. The inside of an empty church at night, with its solemn silence, and the names of people long dead on all sides, is likely to be depressing at any time. In the circumstances Ginger found it definitely uncomfortable.

Tomkins' light flashed several times in the pulpit. Then he rejoined the others. 'Okay,' he said. 'No difficulty.'

Leaving the building and locking the door behind them they returned to the stump by the grave.

'Now compare your prints,' Biggles told Tomkins.

'There's no need,' averred the fingerprint expert. 'I've looked at them under my glass. They were all made by the same man.'

'That's what I expected,' said Biggles.

'Just a minute,' expostulated Gaskin. 'What are you trying to get at?'

'I fancy I've already got to it,' answered Biggles softly. 'Would you mind comparing these prints with those of your unknown burglar? You said you'd got some.'

'Are you suggesting that . . . the parson . . . are you crazy?'

'If you'll do what I tell you, you can answer that question yourself,' murmured Biggles.

Tomkins held a torch while Gaskin, magnifying glass

in hand, obeyed. Suddenly he seemed to stop breathing. For ten seconds silence reigned. Then, in a strange voice he said: 'You're right. In the name of all that's fantastic. The parson . . . a burglar!'

'He's worse than that,' said Biggles grimly. 'I'm afraid he's . . . a murderer.'

Gaskin stared, his jaw sagging. 'You mean. . . .'

'He killed Small. Why, I don't know, but I could make a guess. Having killed him he was faced with the usual difficulty of disposing of the body. Then he had what must have seemed a brain-wave. He decided to bury it.'

'Do you know where?'

'I think so.'

'Where?'

'There.' Biggles pointed.

Gaskin blinked. 'But that's Mrs. Small's grave.'

'I think you'll find that it's also the grave of her son,' said Biggles slowly. 'The body shouldn't be very far down.'

The Inspector drew a deep breath. 'We can soon settle that,' he declared. 'We've got a spade.'

'That's why I told Tomkins to bring it over.'

Gaskin seized the implement.

'This is no place for us,' Biggles told him. 'We'll wait for you at the car.'

*

Twenty minutes later Gaskin joined them. He had recovered his composure. 'You were right,' he said briefly. 'The gun that killed him was on his chest. I shall have to send for help and an ambulance. Looks as if you're going to touch the *Courier* for that thousand.'

Biggles shrugged. 'I'd forgotten about it. As there's

nothing more I can do here we'll drift along home.'

'Just a minute,' requested the Inspector. 'Would you mind telling me how you got on to this?'

'Not at all,' answered Biggles. 'It wasn't difficult. This morning we saw the parson looking for something in the field. This afternoon we found it – or at any rate, something somebody had lost. The mask. That's not a thing an honest man carries about with him. Dewsberry's trouble was, in disposing of Small's body he was working in the dark, and also, we may suppose, in haste. Anyhow, he dropped the mask and it got practically buried. I doubt if we should have noticed it if in his hurry he hadn't buried some of the flowers, too. They told the story. Queer – almost as if Mrs. Small revealed the murderer of her son from the grave.

'I thought that as the churchyard was on Small's beat he wouldn't pass it without looking in. Cigarette ends round this very stump suggested that he had. After that I think the story runs like this. You told us Dewsberry was popular with everyone. It followed that he would be a frequent visitor at the big houses round about. On such visits he would be able, without comment, to go to a bathroom or lavatory, unfasten the window, and make provision for his burglarious return later. He would also have ample opportunity for learning where the valuables were kept. Who would suspect this charming man? On his return home from Clagston Hall with the swag, rather than go near the village he cut across the big field to the churchyard, and so to the house. That's where he he thought he might have dropped his mask. He wouldn't want a thing like that to be found near the rectory. He entered the churchyard through this gate. Small was sitting here on this stump, brooding over his mother.

Being in his dark uniform it's unlikely that Dewsberry would see him.

'What happened after that must remain surmise. Small, of course, would see Dewsberry, but might not have recognized him, for it's hardly likely that the rector would be wearing a garment as conspicuous as a clerical collar. He would see a dark figure come over the stile carrying a bag, and at such a late hour he would either challenge him or follow him. Dewsberry, finding himself discovered, shot Small dead, and buried the weapon with the body, using the spade which was nice and handy in the sexton's shed. We can imagine the state he was in, so it needn't surprise us that he did the job clumsily. He then went home, satisfied in his mind, no doubt, that he would be the last man suspected of being concerned with Small's disappearance.'

'Murder will out,' said the Inspector sententiously. 'What about the plane?'

'That problem shouldn't be difficult to solve,' opined Biggles. 'A reasonable supposition would be that Dewsberry the pilot worked in with his brother, flying the stolen jewels to the Continent. Remember, he's had one conviction for smuggling.'

'That's about it,' agreed Gaskin. 'Sounds simple, the way you put it.'

Biggles smiled. 'That's what Columbus said when he stood an egg on end. I think that's all for tonight. See you later. Come on, Ginger, let's get home.'

7

THE CASE OF THE SECRET INQUISITORS

It was late one night when Biggles received an urgent phone call from his chief, Air Commodore Raymond, head of the Air Section at Scotland Yard. Entering the Yard in the unfamiliar company of its night workers he found the Air Commodore already in conference. The taller of his two companions was introduced as Sir Neville Baker, of the Diplomatic Corps; the other Biggles recognized as Major Charles of M.I.5, counter-espionage section. There was an atmosphere of gravity in the room.

'Sorry to drag you out at this hour,' said the Air Commodore, indicating a chair. 'Charles will explain.'

The Intelligence Officer turned thoughtful eyes on Biggles' face. 'It's a matter that has been worrying us for some time; but the latest development has created a crisis. Briefly, the story is this. For some time past there have been accidents and disappearances involving scientific and political experts of first-rate importance. We can no longer believe that these accidents are unrelated.'

'Two of the men were diplomats,' put in Sir Neville.

'The latest case is that of Maxwell Harrington,' resumed Major Charles.

'A little while ago a few lines crept into the newspapers to the effect that as a geologist Harrington probably knew more than any living man about the mineral deposits of Central and Eastern Europe. That, of course, includes uranium. Harrington disappeared this evening between his hotel and Victoria Station. He was to have taken the boat train for Germany. In the normal course of events we shouldn't have known of his disappearance for something like forty-eight hours; but he had forgotten some documents, so a messenger was sent after him. He was not to be found. Something has happened to him.'

'You mean, you believe he has been abducted?' queried Biggles.

'Yes.'

'If so, the people responsible are probably still unaware that he has been missed,' said Biggles.

'Yes,' agreed Charles. 'In that respect we might be said to be a move ahead of them.'

'What other cases of this sort have there been?' asked Biggles quietly.

Sir Neville answered: 'They have all been comparatively unknown men, but vital brains behind the security of this country. The first was Pierre Lefèbre, a brilliant young French-Canadian who was one of our confidential advisers on the Marshall Plan negotiations. After completing a secret mission to the States he went to Cornwall for a rest. Shortly afterwards his body was washed up at the foot of the cliff in the village where he had been staying. He was in possession of vital information that would be of paramount importance to a hostile power.

But let us move to the more sinister part of the business. It puts abduction and murder in the shade.'

'Would the victims think that?' asked Biggles.

'That's just it. They can't think – those who have been left alive. Adamson, for instance. He directed radio propaganda. He disappeared and was found wandering in Edinburgh. He was completely out of his mind. He has yielded to treatment to some extent, but I doubt if he will ever be able to work for us again, poor fellow.'

'Do you mean, you think we're up against a sort of scientific version of the Grand Inquisition?' questioned Biggles.

'What evidence we have,' replied Major Charles, 'indicates a technique so diabolical that it is difficult to assign it to human agency.'

'All right, sir. Let's have the worst,' requested Biggles.

The Intelligence Officer met his gaze unsmilingly. 'Very well. The worst case so far was that of Peter Bard, Adamson's assistant. He vanished, but turned up again in much the same way as Adamson. There was a difference, however. When we found Adamson his mind was an empty shell. When Bard turned up his mind had not only been emptied, it had been filled up again.' Major Charles paused, choosing his words carefully. 'His whole scale of values and beliefs had been reversed. In other words, he now has a fixed belief in the very propaganda he was supposed to be combating.'

Biggles stared. 'But you can't change a man's mind to that extent – not unless he's willing,' he protested.

Major Charles shrugged. 'Who knows what modern science can do to the human mind, given a sufficiently unscrupulous operator? You may recall the so-called confessions by obviously innocent men, in some of the

European spy trials. This is evidently a development of the same theme.'

'It's true,' affirmed Sir Neville. 'Apart from the danger to our own country, we owe it to humanity to destroy this evil thing.'

Major Charles went on. 'There is money behind the organization. Take the case of Kin Yen. He was a young Chinese aerodynamic expert, temperamental, but of exceptional ability. He was negotiating with us for his own development of the helicopter, simple in principle but remarkably efficient. He disappeared. He's never been found. But we have secret information that a certain foreign power has under trial a prototype of the Yen Helicopter.'

'What was the reason for bringing this case to the Air Police?' inquired Biggles curiously.

'Because we believe that an aircraft may have been employed in the actual kidnapping,' answered Major Charles. 'Poor Adamson raved about a white aeroplane, and still cowers at the sound of an aero-engine. The body of Pierre Lefèbre was so mutilated that the injuries were more consistent with being dropped from an aircraft than falling into the sea from a cliff.'

Biggles stubbed his cigarette thoughtfully. 'Tell me this,' he requested. 'Are you of opinion that the headquarters of this gang – or whatever it is – is somewhere in the British Isles?'

The Air Commodore replied: 'I'm checking up on all airports.'

Major Charles shook his head. 'That's too slow. Harrington is an old man. He couldn't hold out long against his abductors if they applied pressure. Something decisive must be done quickly.'

Biggles toyed with another cigarette. 'I have a feeling that the villain in this case is more likely to be an individual than a foreign government.'

'Then how do you account for what happened with the Yen Helicopter?' countered Charles.

'Inventions can be sold to the highest bidder,' Biggles pointed out.

'What easier way of making big money could there be than by kidnapping a man with a valuable secret, making him divulge it, and then selling it? Again, there may be a man at work who has a mania for power – a sort of second Hitler.'

'You may be right,' conceded Sir Neville.

'Suppose he is? Where is this conjecture getting us?' broke in Major Charles impatiently.

'It narrows our field to an abnormal man working in this country,' answered Biggles. 'Abnormality has its weaknesses – vanity, for instance. Obviously, these victims of kidnapping have to be held in a fit state for questioning – for a time, anyway. I mean, until they have divulged what they know.'

'What exactly are you getting at?' inquired Major Charles.

'I was thinking that it might be possible to plant a fake scientist. He would be in no great danger until he had released his special information.'

Major Charles shook his head. 'I wouldn't ask any man to risk it. Where could we find such a man, anyway?'

'You wouldn't have to go far,' replied Biggles evenly.

They all stared.

'Do you mean ... you'd be willing to try it?' questioned Major Charles.

'Yes.'

'You realize the risk?'

'Of course. But, as you say, we've got to do something, and quickly. I'm not looking for trouble, but the boldest way is often the safest.' Biggles looked at the Air Commodore.

'I imagine you could give me a quick build-up in the Press, as the holder of a top secret? That should be enough to get me kidnapped. You might have me photographed in an unusual get-up, and hint that I have just escaped from behind the Iron Curtain with certain important information.'

'It could be done,' agreed the Air Commodore pensively. 'It should work either way. If a foreign power is behind these kidnappings it would be desperately anxious to recover its secret. If it is an individual he would be interested in acquiring the secret for himself.'

'Quite so,' agreed Biggles. 'All right. Get the story in tomorrow's papers. Then drop it, as if the official censor had stepped in.'

'How do you intend to keep in touch with us?' asked Major Charles.

'That, I'm afraid, would be difficult,' returned Biggles. 'This is a game that can only be played solo. I have one big advantage over the other victims. I do at least know what's likely to happen from the start. I'd like to see the documents covering the previous cases, and any photographs there are available of the people concerned. That's about all I shall need.'

'You'll need a name,' the Air Commodore pointed out.

Biggles smiled. 'What about one in the approved tradition? I suggest Mr. Holmes.'

'Very well,' agreed the Air Commodore grimly. 'We'll see if Mr. Holmes can solve the problem. Are you sure there's nothing else you need?'

'Just a little luck,' answered Biggles, rising.

Somewhat uncomfortable in a suit of old-fashioned style and with some slight alteration to his personal appearance (such as shaving his moustache), Biggles took his breakfast two days later at a West End hotel in which he had booked accommodation.

The day proved to be a tiresome one, because as nothing happened he had ample time to contemplate the hazards of his undertaking. His portrait, with its untruthful caption, had appeared on the previous day in the lunch editions of the London newspapers. He occupied himself with studying reports and photographs relevant to the case.

Evening found him in the hotel lounge glancing through the current issue of *Flight*; and it was while he was thus engaged that he heard a page-boy calling him under the name of Holmes. With a start he remembered that he was Holmes, so beckoning the boy over he took from him the written message that he carried. Ripping open the envelope, he read: 'You are in danger. Do not use the telephone. Report at once to the office.' The message was unsigned.

Biggles tossed his cigarette into the nearest ash-tray, strolled through the foyer and down the hotel steps. A nearby cinema was just emptying and anxious cries of 'Taxi' punctuated the roar of traffic. He hesitated on the kerb, looking to right and left. He appeared to be in luck, for almost at once a taxi pulled in beside him. The driver clicked down his flag. The door swung open. 'Where to, sir?'

'War Office,' answered Biggles as he got in. As the door slammed he sat down, wondering what was going to happen.

He was soon to know. As the seat took his full weight there was a hiss as of escaping steam. So that was it, he thought swiftly, and then smiled faintly. His enemies were not very clever after all, for no agent on the alert would have fallen into a trap as obvious as the taxi.

With the sickly-sweet smell of anaesthetic gas in his nostrils he lost consciousness. . . .

When he opened his eyes again he could see nothing but a large white object. He discovered that he was lying down, and that he was moving. Focusing his eyes with an effort, he made out the white object to be the figure of a nurse. Presently a bell clanged with a familiar note, and he realized that he was in an ambulance. Filtered sunlight streamed in through the frosted windows. The smooth singing of tyres on tarmac told him that he was on a main road. His tried to moisten his lips, which were painfully parched.

'Drink this.' The nurse bent over him with a medicine glass. Her manner was cold and dispassionate.

Biggles behaved as he thought he would be expected to behave. 'Where am I?' he asked. 'What has happened? Was there an accident?'

The nurse answered: 'Yes, an accident. You have been unconscious for some hours. Please lie still.'

'Am I in an ambulance?' inquired Biggles.

'Yes.'

'Where are we going?'

The woman regarded him with something like cynical amusement.

'You are on your way to a private sanatorium.' She

glanced at her watch. 'It is time for another injection,' she announced. 'Don't try to move or speak afterwards, or you will only distress yourself needlessly.'

Biggles did not protest. He felt the stab of a needle in his arm. It was followed by a curious sensation of being held down by invisible weights. He closed his eyes.

Time passed. Biggles lay still, striving, not very successfully, to retain his faculties, for the drug had deprived him of the power of speech and movement. He was conscious, but only just. As in a dream he knew that the ambulance had stopped. The doors were opened. The stretcher on which he lay was eased out. Vaguely against the sky loomed a building of familiar design. It was, he realized with an effort, an airport control-tower. With a feeling of unreality he watched himself being taken through the routine of an outgoing passenger. He was wheeled across the tarmac. A white fuselage, carrying a conspicuous red cross, came into his field of view. A man in a leather flying-jacket was waiting.

'This is Doctor Kahn,' said the nurse softly. 'He flies his own ambulance plane. He is a good pilot. There's no need to worry.'

The doctor followed the stretcher into the cabin. Bending down he took Biggles' pulse, at the same time staring into his eyes. Biggles felt a thrill of loathing. The man's fingers felt like steel encased in a spongy substance.

'Do you suffer from air sickness?'

The doctor's voice had the same intense yet mechanical quality as that of the nurse. 'You can indicate an answer in the affirmative by closing your eyes. Don't try to speak.'

Biggles kept his eyes open. He did not suffer from air sickness.

'Good,' said the doctor. 'We have everything for our patients' comfort.' He dropped Biggles' wrist. 'You are in excellent health, so you will be yourself by the time we arrive.' He left the cabin, and his place was taken by the nurse. The aircraft vibrated as the engine came to life. It taxied out. A minute later it was in the air.

To his great satisfaction Biggles felt his strength returning as the effects of the drug wore off. Altitude may have had something to do with it. Anyway, he was soon able to think more clearly, and by the time the landing wheels bumped the power of movement had returned. He was content with the way things were going – not that there was anything he could do for the time being.

The nurse helped him from the cabin, for he was still shaky. There was a strange whispering in his ears. He thought at first that it must be the after-effects of the drug; but then a salt breeze whipped his face and a gull cried plaintively. It was the sea. He could see it whichever way he looked. There were no trees, only heather in undulating folds, rising on one side to a hill. He supposed that he was on an island, and the heather suggested that it was somewhere off the coast of Scotland.

The nurse propelled him towards a stone-built, castle-like building, dilapidated, and obviously of great age. It was screened by a high wire fence. Near it was a shabby wartime temporary hangar. As they passed it a man came out and walked towards the plane. Looking at him, Biggles saw a round, expressionless face with slanting eyes. He recognized the missing inventor, Kin Yen.

The doctor waited at the fence. With him was a man

dressed as a hospital orderly. 'I'll take over now, Sister,' said the doctor.

They entered the castle, and at the same time stepped into the anaesthetic-smelling atmosphere of a hospital. The door closed behind them with an unpleasant thud of finality.

'A necessary precaution for a private asylum,' said the doctor gravely.

'Are you one of the patients?' inquired Biggles.

'Ah! So you have a warped sense of humour. We shall have to correct that,' murmured the doctor, walking on.

He led the way to a chamber that was something be-tween an office and a consulting-room. The most con-spicuous furniture consisted of a chromium desk and what appeared to be a dentist's chair. The arms were fitted with leather straps. A rubber gag hung from the headpiece.

The doctor took off his flying-kit and hung it in a steel cupboard. 'Make yourself comfortable, Mr. Holmes. You'll find the chair not unpleasant – as long as you don't try to exert yourself.' He seated himself at the desk. Two male attendants appeared from an inner room.

Suddenly the air was stabbed by a blazing white spotlight. The doctor put on a large pair of dark glasses.

Biggles took up an attitude which he thought was ap-propriate to the situation. 'What is this all about?' he demanded. 'I don't understand. I was told there had been an accident. What's going on here?'

'A perfectly natural question, Mr. Holmes,' was the reply. 'I can answer in a few words. I arranged for you to be brought here because I am interested in the same subject as you, notably the mineral deposits of Eastern Europe.'

'Is that all?' Biggles smiled lugubriously. 'Why go to so much trouble about it? I imagine the information I possess is worth something. After all, everybody needs money. I don't know what power you represent, but I'm always anxious to be on the winning side – which means that I'm willing to co-operate, for a consideration.' He sat in the chair and indicated the attendants. 'There's no need for all this theatrical stuff.'

The doctor dismissed the attendants with a wave.

'How wise you are, Mr. Holmes,' said the doctor smoothly. 'But it happens that the organization I represent is not a nation. I stand for a master-group that is interested in revolution in this country. But don't underestimate our strength. It is the strength of supreme intelligence. We do not normally pay for our information.'

'But doesn't that kill the goose that lays the golden eggs as far as their future usefulness is concerned?' questioned Biggles.

The doctor toyed with a gold pencil. 'Not necessarily. We are on the fringe of a field of power undreamed of by ordinary politicians. Already we can empty a man's brain and fill it with ideas of our own choosing. Imagine the possibilities. Certain powers are of course interested in our enterprise.'

'Such as the one that bought the plans of the Yen helicopter,' suggested Biggles.

'Oh, so you know about that?' The doctor dismissed the matter with a wave. 'A mere side-line; a necessity to keep us in funds. We need a certain amount of money, of course. Mr. Kin Yen has, it happens, proved himself useful here as an aircraft mechanic. He has a partiality for opium. That is the only reward he expects for his services. Naturally, we have other means of persuasion. They're quite subtle. Come and see for yourself.' Switching off the spotlight, the doctor led the way to a corridor that brought them to a lift.

'The human brain can be likened to a beautiful but delicate vase,' resumed the doctor as they went up. 'First we learned to empty it. But instead of leaving an empty shell, as in our earlier experiments, we can now refurnish it with whatever ideas we think will be most useful.' He stopped before a door. 'In here we have a man named Harrington in the preliminary stages of being submitted to the Superior Will. The secrets he will give us will provide us with enough money to run this establishment for a further twelve months. In view of his age, I'm afraid the final stage of re-education will scarcely be worth while.' The doctor opened the door.

With an involuntary tightening of the muscles, Biggles saw, between two white-robed attendants, an old man whose hair gleamed silver under blazing spotlights.

'Tonight he will be allowed to rest,' murmured the doctor. 'Tomorrow I shall extract his secrets.'

When, a few moments later, the doctor took him back to the consulting-room, Biggles was cold with suppressed anger. But that did not prevent his brain from working smoothly. He had an idea. He was, he realized, dealing with a man who, if not mad, was on the borderline of insanity. And, as he had suspected, his driving force, as with most seekers after power, was vanity. He looked around. They were alone.

'I gather you enjoy your work?' he remarked, seating himself uninvited in the sinister chair.

'It is for the master-group,' answered the doctor

casually. 'Eventually we shall control the world. We have no feelings beyond that.'

'That infernal drug of yours has made me thirsty,' said Biggles, changing the subject. 'Am I allowed to have a drink?'

'Certainly. Wine or water?' inquired the doctor, picking up an intercommunication telephone.

The doctor gave an order over the phone in a language unknown to Biggles. Almost at once a little ape-faced man came in with a glass of water which he put on a stand at Biggles' elbow. Having done this he retired silently.

'Aren't you afraid of being left alone with me?' queried Biggles, as he picked up the glass.

The doctor frowned. 'Afraid? Control, my dear sir, is always a matter of superior intelligence.' He took from a drawer of his desk what appeared to be a fountain-pen. 'One spot of the chemical contained in this cylinder and you would know nothing for a long time,' he boasted.

Biggles took a gulp of water. The next second he had stiffened, gasping. The glass crashed on the floor as his hands flew to his throat. His head sagged forward. 'You devil!' he panted. 'You've poisoned me.'

'The fools!' snapped the doctor, and, springing to his feet, tried to catch Biggles as he fell.

In a flash Biggles had him in a stranglehold, one hand twisting the wrist that held the weapon. It fell with a clatter. Biggles snatched it up, and turning it on the gasping doctor depressed the switch. There was a hiss like that made by a soda-water siphon, and the struggling figure collapsed. Breathing heavily from his efforts, Biggles dragged the man into the chair, strapped him in and threw a towel over the pallid face, having first removed the dark glasses.

He fitted the glasses on his own face. Then, moving swiftly, he went to the cupboard and took out the doctor's flying-kit. With the secret weapon still in his hand he walked to the door and looked out. Seeing no one, he strode on to the front door. An attendant, seeing him coming, hurried to open the gate in the fence. The air ambulance was still standing outside the hangar, with its mechanic, Yen, leaning against the fuselage as if waiting for orders.

'Get in,' Biggles told him curtly.

The Chinaman obeyed without question. Biggles climbed into the pilot's seat. Three minutes later he was in the air.

The sun was sinking into the Atlantic when the ambulance plane returned. A man in a white coat raced towards it. 'Doctor, there has been an escape!' he shouted. 'I've switched on the high-tension in the fence –'

By that time Biggles had jumped down. He held an automatic. 'Switch it off again,' he ordered crisply.

The man's mouth fell open in dismay as the aircraft disgorged a load of armed police officers. Air Commodore Raymond was among them. He joined Biggles, who ran on to the building.

Policemen poured down the corridors.

'All right, Bigglesworth, we can leave the rest to them,' asserted the Air Commodore.

As they watched, policemen began to emerge with their prisoners. The doctor and the nurse were among them. A police Auster aircraft was just landing.

'There's no need for you to stay if you don't want to,'

the Air Commodore told Biggles. 'It'll take some time to clean up this place. I expect I shall be here all night. More than anything I'm concerned with any victims of this bunch of lunatics, who may be here.'

'Well, if you can manage without me, I'll get along,' answered Biggles. 'That will be Ginger just landing in the Auster. He'll take me home. I've had a pretty hectic day. I'll let you have a full report tomorrow.'

'Good enough,' agreed the Air Commodore.

Lighting a cigarette, Biggles walked towards the Auster.

8

OPERATION STARLIGHT

AT ten thousand feet the Air Police Auster droned a lonely course across the indigo bowl that was the earth. Above, the midnight sky was spangled with a million stars. Below, the world that no longer sleeps was studded with a million sparks of light.

At the controls, on a seat-parachute, his face ghastly in the reflected glow of the instrument panel, sat Air-Detective Inspector Bigglesworth. Beside him at the dual controls, half-masked with high frequency radio equipment, was his second-in-command, Police Pilot 'Algy' Lacey. Behind were the two other members of the Special Air Police, 'Bertie' Lissie and 'Ginger' Hebblethwaite, also wearing parachutes. No one spoke. Expressions were grim, for upon the outcome of the night's work, they had been warned, might depend the career of their chief, Air Commodore Raymond at Scotland Yard.

All were indignant at the criticism being voiced by those in high places who seemed unable to appreciate the difficulties of preventing aircraft from being used for those unlawful transactions which world conditions and high profits invited. H.M. Customs and Excise complained of illegal movements of diamonds, furs and drugs. The Currency Control Commission alleged the

unauthorized transfer of money to and from the
Continent. Security Intelligence suspected that secret
agents were coming and going without passport examination. Radar stations were reporting unidentified
aircraft, mostly by night.

Biggles did not dispute this. He knew through con-
tinental colleagues that every country in Western Europe
was faced by the same problem. He also knew the
limitations of aircraft in counter measures. A suspicious
vehicle on the road can be halted and examined. A ship
can be held and searched. But an aircraft cannot be
stopped without employing methods which, common in
war, would be held inexcusable in peace time. To main-
tain a constant patrol over every coast and frontier was
out of the question.

Biggles had received permission to employ unorthodox methods if he wished, and these, with the co-
operation of radar stations, were now in action. For a
week he had drawn blank. This was his last chance, for
ground forces protested they could not stand by
indefinitely.

'Here we are,' announced Algy sharply. 'Okay. Go
ahead,' he told the distant radar operator. For
some ten seconds he listened. Then, half turning
to Biggles, he went on: 'Unidentified aircraft gliding
in over Suffolk coast. Course, west-north-west.
Height eight thousand. No navigation lights. Ignores
signals.'

Biggles pulled the Auster round, nose down, throttle
wide open for speed.

Algy spoke again. 'Northerly – northerly – hold it.
Should intercept at forty miles.'

Three minutes passed. 'Bandit changing course –

westerly,' report Algy, still taking signals. 'He's losing height.'

Biggles was staring ahead, eyes scanning the sky for the glow of an exhaust, which alone betrays a darkened aircraft at night.

'Getting close,' said Algy tensely. 'There he is – half left. Going down.'

'I've got him,' answered Biggles, swinging round and side-slipping steeply to get in the blind spot of the objective aircraft. 'Looks like a helicopter. Hello! There go the landing lights. Someone was expecting him. I make 'em on Brandon Heath. See the Brandon-Thetford road. Plenty of room to get down there. Take over. Give Raymond the pin-point. Glide on as far as you can to give us a chance to get at 'em before they hear you. Hold her steady.'

Biggles raised the flap seat and moved aft. 'This is it,' he told Ginger and Bertie. 'I'll go first. Follow fast. We're down to two thousand so don't hold it too long.' Opening the escape hatch he gripped the ring of his parachute and dived into the void.

Ginger and Bertie followed in quick succession.

As he plummeted through space, Ginger saw the landing light go out. He counted five, pulled, and a moment later was floating in space, gathering himself for the shock of landing. He fell, but was up in an instant, slipping his harness. Fifty yards away another brolly was collapsing. A dark figure broke from it. They met. It was Bertie.

Racing over rough grass and heather towards the sound of an idling aero engine they overtook Biggles and hurried on together, keeping the silhouette of the helicopter between them and a house beyond. When they reached it a man in the cockpit was handing out parcels to two men on the ground.

'Stand still,' ordered Biggles crisply. 'We're police –'

There was a shout of alarm and a curse. A gun spat. Biggles returned the shot and one of the two men fell. The other started to run. Bertie tripped him. The helicopter's engine roared. 'Stop him,' rapped out Biggles, and Ginger emptied his gun at the rotor blades. Splinters flew. The engine, relieved of its load, raced, forcing the pilot to switch off. Biggles ordered him to get down, and the man, having no means of escape, complied. He glanced at the bundles on the ground and shrugged. 'I reckon Alex tipped you off about –'

Half an hour later two police cars arrived. Air Commodore Raymond and some plain clothes men got out. 'Nice work, Bigglesworth,' congratulated the Air Commodore. 'What have you caught?'

Biggles smiled, faintly. 'Judging from their weight, enough watches to make a free issue to the Force.'

Statements made by the helicopter pilot caught in the act of smuggling the watches confirmed what Biggles had suspected: that more than one organization was making a good thing out of illegal air transportation. As usual with gangsterism these were now in conflict with each other, to the danger of the public who little suspected what was going on over their heads. Obviously, behind these transactions were men with brains, air experience and big money available.

It seemed unlikely that such men would take part in actual operations. They would keep in the background. Should their agents be caught they could be replaced. Biggles' problem was how to get at them. He knew the nickname of one – Alex – let slip by the helicopter pilot, who turned out to be an ex-officer dismissed the Service for personal smuggling on operational flights. He stated that he had been approached immediately after his court-martial by a man unknown to him. Hc was, of course, an ideal type for the smugglers – efficient, resentful, and now out of a job. Thinking on these lines Biggles had baited a trap.

Algy, under the assumed name of Mason, had just been cashiered for improper conduct – or so a notice, with a photo, in the press announced. A week had passed. Biggles waited in the Air Police Ops. Room for developments. Algy loafed about the West End, keeping away from Scotland Yard.

On the morning of the eighth day Biggles' 'phone rang. As he listened his eyelids made a signal to Bertie and Ginger who were watching. 'Great work, Algy,' he said at last. 'Accept, but don't appear too anxious. We'll be there. I'll warn Marcel Brissac of the Sûreté to stand by.' He hung up, and turning to the others explained. 'It's worked. Algy has been offered a hundred pounds to fly a Puss Moth to France tonight. All he knows is he's to land a passenger and bring a parcel home. His starting point and objective will be given him at zero hour. He thinks the machine must be kept near London.'

'What's our drill?' inquired Ginger.

'He's going to make a forced landing on the Downs north-west of Brighton. When we hear him coming, fiddling with his engine, we flash our code cypher with hand torches and he'll touch down as near to us as possible.'

'What will his passenger say when Algy says he's going to land?'

'What can he say? Carry on over the Ditch with a

sticky engine? Not likely. Obviously he's not a pilot or he wouldn't need one. For that reason he won't dare to interfere with Algy for fear of a crack-up. We'll go down by road. Let's get mobile and find a good spot.'

Biggles and his party were in position by nightfall. Conditions were perfect. Visibility was good. There was no wind, no moon. They waited. A distant village clock struck the hours. Occasionally a big machine of one of the regular services droned over.

It was not until two a.m. that they heard the sound for which they were listening – the purr of a light plane apparently having trouble with its engine.

'Lights,' ordered Biggles crisply.

Bertie and Ginger dashed off to their prearranged stations, torches winking the police call sign. They couldn't see the machine for it carried no lights, but they could follow the sound as it lost height. Then, suddenly, it loomed up, and those on the ground converged at a run on the spot where trundling wheels announced that it was on the ground. They found it on the fairway of a golf-course, for Algy had overshot a little, excusable in the circumstances.

Two men were standing beside the Moth when they arrived. One was Algy. The other, carrying a small suit-case, was, judging from his language, in a flaring temper. Curiously enough he took little notice of the new arrivals until Biggles said, cheerfully: 'Hello! Having a spot of trouble?'

The unknown man spun round. 'How far am I from a road and where can I get a car?' he demanded harshly.

'I've got one waiting,' answered Biggles evenly. 'We're police officers. Better come quietly. I'll take the bag.'

That did it. There was a struggle, but the odds were four to one and the handcuffs soon clicked.

'Let's see what's in the bag,' said Biggles. 'Show a light, someone.'

Ginger's torch flashed on a mixed collection of jewellery.

'Looks like the swag of the Grosvenor Square raid last week,' observed Biggles. 'Inspector Gaskin will be tickled to death to see this.' He looked up. 'How much did you pay for this trip?'

'Five hundred,' grated the man. 'He told me it was safe. I'll get him for this.'

'Tell us who he was and *we'll* get him,' suggested Biggles.

Inspector Gaskin and his men, who had been waiting in a police car on the road, bustled up. 'Well – well. If if isn't Carlo the Cat!' he exclaimed delightedly.

'He's all yours,' murmured Biggles. 'I've more work to do. You can have the sparklers but I shall need the case.'

'Where are you going?'

'France.' Biggles touched the aircraft. 'In this. See you later.'

After Inspector Gaskin and his prisoner had gone, still standing by the captured Puss Moth Biggles spoke to Algy. 'Now give us the gen.' Algy complied. 'I was picked up by a Rolls at ten o'clock outside the Aero Club as arranged and driven to a farm on the south side of Ashdown Forest. There couldn't be any secret about the place because after the trip to France I had to fly back.'

'You could find it again – on the ground?'

'Easily. The chap who had spoken to me in London

was waiting. He wore a mask but I knew the voice. I'll tell you about him later. My orders were to fly a passenger to Beauvais. On the road that crosses the open country beyond the ridge where the R.101 crashed a car would be waiting, making a flare path with its headlights. I was to land my passenger, collect a parcel and come home. Three blips of the engine would be the signal for landing lights to be switched on for me. The Puss lives in a barn beside a grass field of about fifty acres – ideal for the job.'

'I take it the machine's all right?'

'Right as rain.'

'Fine. Now, this is the drill. You'll take the car home. Bertie with you, because as the machine started with two up it had better not land with three – in case the gang are in touch by 'phone or radio. Stop at the first 'phone box and tell the Air Commodore what's happened. He said he'd wait. I want him to call Marcel Brissac of the Sûreté, who's standing by, and ask him to rush a car to Beauvais in case we need help. On his side of the Channel it's his pigeon, anyway. If all goes well there I shall fly straight back to this Ashdown Forest landing ground. You'll take the Chief there and wait handy to raid the place as soon as I'm on the ground. That's about all.'

Algy nodded. 'Okay. We'll move off. Don't forget to blip your engine for the landing lights.' He went off, Bertie with him.

'I'll have a cigarette,' Biggles told Ginger. 'We must give Marcel time to get to Beauvais. With any luck tonight we may land one of the big fish. The thing is to work fast before they realize what's happening. Tomorrow we'll see in whose name this Puss was registered.'

Presently they took their places in the machine and headed south across the Channel, keeping clear of an occasional regular service aircraft. The flight was without incident. There was no difficulty in finding the rendezvous for Beauvais is a well-known landmark. Across the vast, flat hedgeless fields that are a feature of Northern France, the road to the south showed like a grey tape. Beside it, the headlights of a stationary car, at right-angles to the road, could be seen from a long way off – the only lights in the sleeping countryside.

Biggles did not go straight down. He held on a little way until, far to the south, appeared the lights of a solitary vehicle racing north. 'That should be Marcel,' he observed.

Turning, he cut his engine and circled in a slow glide, keeping the objective car in the centre. In this way he was some minutes getting down, finishing his run in the flare path a hundred yards from the source of light. He taxied nearer, switched off, and with the suitcase in his hand, jumped down. Ginger followed. As they walked on to the car the headlights dimmed. Three men stood waiting.

'Everything all right?' inquired a voice, in English.

'Why not?'

'You were a long time getting down.'

'No hurry, was there?'

'Where's the stuff?'

'Here.' Biggles held up the case.

'Hand it over.' The order was peremptory.

Biggles' surprise was genuine. 'What's the idea?'

'This.'

Biggles stared into the muzzle of an automatic. The bag was snatched from him. 'So that's it,' he said grimly.

'You offer people a trip over and frame' em when they arrive. How do I get to Paris?'

'You've got legs.'

'I was told –'

'We'd bring you over. Okay. So you're here. Quit bleating.'

'Get the stuff, Alex,' said one of the others. 'We don't want the case.'

The bag was opened. There was a brief brittle silence. 'Empty,' rasped Alex. He turned on Biggles. 'Where's the stuff?'

'Looks as if we've both been double-crossed,' answered Biggles evenly.

Ginger, playing for time, cut in. 'Leave me out of this. There's a parcel to go back. Hand it over and I'll leave you to it.'

He was handed a brown paper bundle.

'Wait for this car to go past before you start up,' ordered Alex.

The car came on; but it didn't go past. With a screech of brakes it skidded to a stop, disgorging gendarmes, and before the smugglers could really have grasped what was happening they were seized. A gun cracked but no one was hit.

'*Voila!* Beegles, old fox, we arrive on the dots,' greeted Marcel. 'What do we catch?'

'A very dirty line in crooks.'

'*Bon*. We clean them up. Do you come to Paris?'

'I'd love to, but I haven't time. I want to get back to the other end of this little shuttle service right away. Before I go we'd better have a look at this.'

Ginger's parcel was opened. Bundles of bank-notes fell out.

'These must stay in France,' declared Marcel.

'As you say,' agreed Biggles. 'It's your country. Ring me tomorrow at the Yard and we'll check the details. Take care of Alex. So long. Come on, Ginger.'

The run back from France to the Sussex depot of the secret air operators provided Biggles with an opportunity to discuss with Ginger the information gained from the night's work. The picture, he averred, was still not clear. He had not been surprised to find the man Alex at Beauvais. What had confused the issue was the double-crossing of their customers by the gang. That didn't fit. How long, he asked Ginger, could they hope to get away with that sort of treachery? The transportation of international jewel thieves was understandable; but once word leaked out in the underworld that the air service was a racket to relieve them of their ill-gotten gains, not only would that source of revenue dry up but retribution would follow.

Another point. It seemed that there was nothing permanent about the landing arrangements in France, probably because there were so many districts where it would be possible for a small aircraft to get down. The location could be changed constantly, setting the police the impossible task of guessing the next. There would, of course, have to be a base somewhere for servicing and maintenance. The Ashdown Forest site might be one. 'We shall see,' concluded Biggles, as he glided across the south coast and headed for their objective.

There were not many lights about, for it was now the dark hour before the dawn. Visibility remained good, and the Forest, cut into jig-saw sections by roads, lay like a stain across the face of rural Sussex. Taking a course along the southern fringe Biggles blipped his engine three times. Instantly four orange lights, in the form of a letter L, marked the landing strip.

'That was easier than I expected,' murmured Biggles, cutting his engine and S turning to drop off height without losing sight of the markers. He pointed to twin red lights moving slowly along a road a mile away. 'There's the Air Commodore,' he remarked. 'That big house near the landing strip must be part of the set-up. We may have a hot few minutes before the Chief arrives. When the operator below sees me instead of Algy he'll know something's wrong. It should take him a few seconds to get over the shock. That'll be our chance to catch him on one foot. When I get out, you lie doggo ready to take a hand should anyone reach for a gun. Okay. Here we go.'

Biggles glided in to an easy landing on a fair surface. The landing lights died at once. A torch blinked. Behind it loomed a big modern field barn. The double doors gaped open. Lights inside revealed benches, tools, oil drums. A man, beckoning, retired into it. Biggles followed and switched off. Without haste he got down, moved clear of the machine, then turned sharply to face a masked operator.

The shock that he had predicted caused the man to stiffen, staring, mute. Recovering, his right hand flashed to a side pocket.

'Don't do anything silly,' advised Biggles calmly. 'I'm not alone.'

Instinctively the man snatched a glance over his shoulder and looked into Ginger's gun. Turning back he stammered: 'Who – who are you?'

'Police. The game's up. Don't make matters worse by losing your head.'

'But where's my pilot?'

'He's all right. Actually, he's one of mine. Take that mask off. You don't need it now.'

When the man obeyed it was Biggles' turn to stare. 'I know you,' he said slowly. 'Group Captain – Brail! Are you out of your mind?'

'Probably. I remember you, too, now. Bigglesworth. I heard you were something to do with the police.'

'How did you get mixed up in a show like this?'

'The old story. After I retired I started gambling. When I went broke a man came along and offered me a job in a private air concern. It sounded interesting – and easy money.'

'Too easy,' murmured Biggles. 'What exactly have you been doing?'

'Acting as station commander here. I guessed there was a little quiet smuggling going on – nothing serious.'

'If nothing serious why reach for a gun?'

'We've had a spot of bother with an opposition concern run by an American tough named Alex. I thought you might be him.'

'Alex met the 'plane at Beauvais. Gave me a parcel of notes to bring back.'

Brail started. 'Where is it?'

'The French police have got it.'

Brail spoke earnestly. 'If Alex gave you notes they'd be duds, with a time bomb in one of the packets. He's already killed one of our pilots that way.'

'But how could he know of your arrangements?'

'He's got spies everywhere.'

Biggles turned to Ginger. 'Go to the house and 'phone the Yard. Ask them to put you through to the Sûreté on the private line and warn them about a possible bomb in that parcel. Hurry.'

Ginger dashed off.

To Brail, Biggles said, 'You know the man you sent to France last night?'

'No. I don't ask questions.'

'He was a cracksman with a load of stolen jewellery.'

Brail made a gesture of resignation. 'In that case it looks as if I've had it. All right. I may have been a dupe but I won't be a scapegoat. I'm ready to talk any time you like.'

The Air Commodore, with Algy and Bertie, strode in.

'Here's my Chief,' said Biggles. 'Talk to him.'

Ten minutes later Ginger came back. 'Marcel's all right,' he reported. 'There was a bomb in the parcel. When Alex found himself in the same car with it he had to open up.'

'Let's get along,' said the Air Commodore. 'Inspector Gaskin can look after things here.'

*

Group Captain Brail, arrested while in charge of the unauthorized landing strip in Sussex, angry at being duped and no doubt hoping to get off lightly by turning Queen's Evidence (which, his service record being taken into account, he did), had plenty to say. Incidentally, his male staff in the house (he was a bachelor) were ex-service mechanics, but they knew nothing about what was really going on.

At one time the man for whom he worked, an international adventurer who called himself Luftmann, had the sky to himself. With headquarters in Switzerland, his business was smuggling light-weight, high-duty merchandise, and currency. This, obviously, had developed into something more ambitious. Alex had been one of his men, but having been sacked for pilfering had started on his own account, working from Paris. Naturally, the two gangs had clashed.

There was no dearth of war-trained pilots in Europe. The pay was high and the work was regarded as safe, for these airmen knew better than anyone that it was practically impossible for any country to mount an adequate guard on every field on which an aircraft might land, or on which non-fragile goods could be dropped by parachute, as sometimes happened.

Brail stated that outside these two smuggling enterprises there was reason to believe that a more sinister service was at work moving personnel; for Luftmann's pilots, night-flying without lights, had reported near-collisions with another unlighted aircraft. In fact, one of these pilots had been shot at when he nearly rammed this aircraft standing on the sands of The Wash at low tide – for which reason Luftmann no longer used that particular landing ground.

Of particular interest to Biggles was the information that Luftmann gave his orders to Brail over the 'phone. But this form of communication was one way only. If Brail had anything to report he had to send a cable to an address in Geneva. Luftmann would then 'phone him, all conversations beginning with an exchange of passwords. These Brail revealed. Luftmann rarely came to England. When he did he came over on the regular service and motored down from London.

Biggles summed up with the Air Commodore. Now that Alex was out of it the surviving members of his gang would probably take fright and disperse. The next man to get was Luftmann. The address in Geneva was probably an accommodation one. The thing was to get the man to England. A cable could be sent. When Luftmann 'phoned he could be told that serious trouble was brewing and he had better come over.

'Even if he doesn't come himself he'll send someone,' declared Biggles. 'If we can go on nibbling bits off his organization it'll shake him – and his pilots, who'll wonder what they're running into.'

The Air Commodore agreed.

The cable was sent from Forest Row. Biggles, Ginger and Bertie took up residence in the now empty house by the landing strip, Algy having been detailed to reconnoitre the sands of The Wash for wheel tracks. Biggles sat by the telephone.

The call from Luftmann came through at ten the same night. The passwords were exchanged, Biggles imitating Brail's voice as well as he could. He was smiling when he hung up. 'He says he'll be here at noon tomorrow,' he told the others. 'We might as well go to bed.'

*

Eleven o'clock the following morning saw a reception party in position, Biggles having been reinforced by plain clothes men from the Yard. These remained out of sight.

At eleven-fifty, Ginger, who had been watching from an upstairs window, reported a Rolls coming down the road. It turned in the drive and stopped at the front door, which had been left open. Three men got out. One was short, burly, sleek and immaculate. The others, acting like bodyguards, were rough types. Together they strode into the lounge where Biggles was seated at Brail's desk.

'Who are you?' demanded the well-dressed man, speaking with a pronounced accent. 'Where's Brail?'

'He's been unavoidably detained,' answered Biggles smoothly. 'Are you Mr. Luftmann?'

'Yes. I was Luftmann. I speak with Brail last night. He say he has something important to tell me.'

'Actually, you spoke to me,' corrected Biggles. 'And what I have to tell you is this. The man you arranged to fly to France two nights ago is in prison, and very angry. Your traffic manager here is also under arrest. Between them they have told us quite a lot about you, with the result that you, too, are under arrest.'

Luftmann was staring stupidly, jaw sagging.

'To save unpleasantness I should tell you that this house is cordoned off by police, so resistance on your part will serve no useful purpose,' went on Biggles imperturbably. 'Finally, I must warn you that anything you say may be used as evidence against you.'

Luftmann choked something in a foreign language. His companions drew pistols and started backing towards the door, eyes active.

'Drop those guns,' ordered Biggles sternly. 'Shoot a policeman in this country and you'll hang, I promise you.'

He ducked as one of the bodyguards took deliberate aim at him. But the shot was never fired. Through every door surged policemen.

Luftmann, ashen, dropped into a chair. 'I can explain this,' he cried desperately.

'I doubt it,' replied Biggles dryly. He turned to the

Air Commodore who now walked in. 'I think Mr. Luftmann wants to make a statement, sir.'

But Mr. Luftmann had fainted.

*

For a week Algy and Bertie had taken turns to patrol at dawn the wide sands of The Wash after low tides had occurred during the night. So far they had not seen a mark. Radar had nothing to report.

The purpose of these flights was to ascertain if the sands were still being used as a landing ground by un-registered aircraft, and if so, the precise spot where the landings were made. Also, by examination of the tracks, perhaps identify the type of aircraft being used.

Conditions were now near perfect: the weather, the moon, the wind and the time of low tide, all were right, so on his next patrol Algy was not surprised to find what he sought. As he sideslipped steeply towards twin sets of double wheel tracks he realized how well chosen was the spot for what was going on. The sands stretched for miles without an obstruction. Towards the tracks at almost unbelievable speed raced the incoming tide, each wave was overlapping the last, so that in a matter of minutes the tell-tale marks would be erased.

When he landed the advancing water was a mile away, yet even so he had barely time to finish what he wanted to do. In fact, at the end he had to run for it, and, with the water at his wheels, take off in a cloud of spray.

An hour later he was reporting to Biggles in the Ops. Room. 'The machine that landed on those sands last night was no type I've ever seen or heard of,' he de-clared. 'It had double tyres on each leg of the undercart and the tyres had no tread pattern. The wheel track was ten feet three and a half inches. The machine had a fixed tail skid yet it could turn in its own length, which means at least twin power units.'

Biggles drew thoughtfully on his cigarette. 'I'd say that machine was equipped for the job – designed to tell anyone who saw its tracks precisely nothing. No treads. Why? Because the tread of a tyre names its maker. As individuals can't build special machines it must have government backing. Which government? Your guess is as good as mine. With conditions perfect it should be here again within a day or two – or not for another month. The question is how to catch it in the act – bearing in mind that the crew carry guns.'

'What about laying on the brolly act?' suggested Bertie.

'Too dangerous. Don't forget what happened to King John. When I land I want to be able to get off again.'

'To land in a machine will be asking to be shot up,' Ginger pointed out.

'That's a game that two can play. If I had my way I'd shoot these sneak raiders out of the sky; they're a menace to honest pilots; but of course the Chief won't hear of that.'

'So we have to let them shoot at us before we can shoot back,' murmured Bertie. 'Jolly good.'

'All we can do is sit around on the coast, and when we hear this prowler come in, fly out and make a grab at him – or something of that sort. I'll think about it. We start tonight.'

'What do you suppose this machine's doing?' queried Ginger.

'Putting down somebody who prefers not to come into the country through a normal port of entry. Which means we've got to be careful not to start an international rumpus.'

'Let's catch these birds for a start,' suggested Bertie.

For three nights the police Auster, based on an R.A.F. station in Lincolnshire, watched and waited by the sands, standing at alert only when landings were possible. Two watchers from the Security Division were on duty on the Norfolk side, in touch by high frequency radio.

The fourth night came, with the moon riding high and shreds of cloud being hounded across the sky by a stiffish easterly wind. The tide had ebbed, leaving a vast grey plain of glistening sand with here and there a sheet of shallow water from which was wafted the reek of seaweed and the melancholy cries of gulls.

Biggles looked at his watch. 'Low water,' he remarked. 'If they're coming it should be soon.'

Hardly had the words left his lips when all were brought to their feet by the drone of aero engines, the sound seeming to come from the sea.

'He's coming in low to beat radar,' said Biggles. 'Okay, let's go.'

*

Almost at once it was possible to see the machine, black against the pallid background, the only moving thing in a scene that was as lifeless as a picture. It turned into wind, slowed to a crawl, stopped.

'We've got 'em, the fools,' muttered Biggles, racing for the spot. 'They daren't take off down-wind in this breeze, and they haven't room to get off into it without hitting that pool of stagnant water. Have the gun ready, Algy,' he ordered, as he throttled back and swung round to make his approach from behind.

Another minute and his wheels were grumbling as, tail up, he sped to close the gap. Only at the last moment, as the tail dropped and dragged, did he turn broadside on to enable Algy to bring a Sten gun to bear.

Jabbing flecks of flame and the vicious smack of bullets told Ginger they were under fire. Algy's gun chattered and the target began to move.

What followed provided a subject for argument for weeks to come. The pilot tried to take off. So much was apparent. Whether he was hit by one of Algy's shots; whether he had forgotten the pool in front of him or was blinded by the reflection of the moon on it; whether he struck a patch of soft sand or lost his nerve were all matters for surmise. What certainly happened was, the machine, running tail up, suddenly tried to turn. No undercarriage, designed for forward movement only, could be expected to stand up to such a cross-strain. It collapsed. A wing tip tore into the sand. The machine cart-wheeled, and was in flames before it had stopped rolling.

Without fire-fighting appliances there was no question of rescue.

For Biggles it was a disappointing end to the affair, for it left the identity of the aircraft, and its occupants, unrevealed.

The sands were watched for weeks, but there were no more visitors.

These are other Knight Books

FIRST BBC TV TOP OF THE FORM
  QUIZ BOOK

SECOND BBC TV TOP OF THE FORM
  QUIZ BOOK

Two books of the television programme
that now spans the globe – books that will
give the reader hours of entertainment,
while he teaches himself about the world
around us, and tests his wits.

Compiled by the programme's Question
Setter, Boswell Taylor, each book contains
over 700 questions and full answers on
dozens of different subjects

Ask your local bookseller, or at your public
library, for details of other Knight Books,
or write to the Editor-in-Chief, Knight
Books, Arlen House, Salisbury Road,
Leicester. LE1 7QS.